THE BRIDE IS MISSING

Cat is meant to be marrying Stephen after a whirlwind romance. So why is she now waking up on a small Welsh island, still in her hen party outfit? She initially thinks it's a pre-wedding prank — but soon it becomes apparent that the reality is much more sinister. Along with Greg, the man who discovered her when she woke by the beach, Cat is drawn into the web of intrigue which has entangled both her fiancé and her best friend . . .

Books by Anne Hewland
in the Linford Romance Library:

ANNE HEWLAND

---◆---

THE BRIDE IS MISSING

Complete and Unabridged

LINFORD
Leicester

First published in Great Britain in 2019

First Linford Edition
published 2020

*A catalogue record for this book is available
from the British Library.*

ISBN 978–1–4448–4577–8

Published by
Ulverscroft Limited
Anstey, Leicestershire

Set by Words & Graphics Ltd.
Anstey, Leicestershire
Printed and bound in Great Britain by
T. J. International Ltd., Padstow, Cornwall

This book is printed on acid-free paper

1

Cat opened her eyes. Something was wrong — very wrong. She was lying on a narrow bed, dressed but bare-footed and covered with a rough grey blanket. Beyond her feet, sun shone through a small square window, showing an impossibly blue sea.

Was this an island? Was she on holiday? She should have been on holiday — and not just any holiday, her honeymoon.

She struggled up onto her elbows, her head swimming with the effort. Down on the beach, a dark figure was moving, silhouetted against the azure waves.

She frowned. That wasn't Stephen, was it? It should have been Stephen.

Where is he? she thought. *How did I get here? We must have got married already. But I don't remember that happening.*

It was all too much to work out. But some deep instinct told her that she was safe here. All she wanted to do was sleep. She didn't want to think about Stephen. She just wanted to forget him . . .

When she woke again, the sun had moved round, casting the longer shadows of late afternoon. How wonderful it would be, to sleep here forever, in this beautiful place. Nothing to worry about. Losing herself in dreams.

She had always dreamed of working somewhere like this. Conservation, helping the planet. But that dream had never seemed so far away.

Forget the dreams — she had to wake up. She knew this time that sinking back into oblivion wasn't possible.

She sat up carefully, wincing at her aching head.

'So you're awake.' The voice was abrupt.

Her head jerked round and she winced again. He was standing in the

2

doorway with the brightness of the sun behind him. She could hardly see him.

'Yes.'

'I left you water. You haven't touched it.'

She turned to look where he was pointing. Yes, there was a bottle of water on a rough wooden box beside her. A makeshift bedside table. She realised now that her mouth was painfully dry.

'Sorry — I didn't see it.' She reached over, wincing again and hoping he hadn't noticed. She didn't want to look as if she was playing for sympathy. She unscrewed the top, gulping it down. The top had loosened easily. Perhaps it had been refilled with tap water.

He had made no move to help her.

'That's the only way to deal with a hangover.'

He didn't sound sympathetic.

'Hangover? It can't be.' Whatever was affecting her, it couldn't be that. 'I'm not allowed to drink. I'm on long-term medication.'

He shrugged. 'Whatever.'

3

Obviously he didn't believe her. Why should he? But there could be no exceptions — ever. Even on her hen night. Because Amanda would have made certain she didn't.

Amanda would have taken care of her, watched over her. Cat would have done the same for her, if she'd had to. She could rely on Amanda — she always had done . . . She closed her eyes again.

He said abruptly, 'Hey, don't go to sleep on me again. We have to decide what to do about you. When I found you, crumpled in the doorway, you said you didn't know why you were here or who you are. That's what you said.' He didn't sound convinced. 'Has anything come back to you?'

'No,' she said slowly. 'I'll have to stay here, won't I? Until I remember. I won't get in the way.'

It might work. Just to give her time to think things through. Because whatever she had told this man at the start, it was all sweeping back now. A huge dark cloud of everything she didn't want to remember. She had made a huge mess of everything.

She was going to marry Stephen. It was a whirlwind romance. She had been swept away by how vulnerable he had been. She had promised . . . Somehow, however, whatever had gone on in her head during her enforced period of oblivion, she was now seeing everything with a new clarity. She had made a terrible mistake.

'Convenient,' her rescuer said. She supposed she could call him that. He could have been reading her mind. She wanted to go back to the blissfulness of not knowing. To stay here, lost to it all. That way, perhaps she could miss the wedding altogether.

Perhaps she already had. How long had she been asleep? And it hadn't been her fault. Just a bit longer — until her head stopped aching and she could decide what to do for the best.

He came into the room. She could see what he looked like for the first time. He had dark, tangled hair and a tanned, strong face. He was frowning, dark brows coming together in a way that seemed almost sinister.

She said firmly, 'I don't know you. I have no idea where we are or how I got here.'

Crumpled in the doorway? It was as if she had been left for him to find. But she didn't remember anything about that.

'So you say. But that's not what your eyes are telling me. Your face is too expressive. If I were you, I would remember that when you're lying in future.'

'I'm sure we've never met. I would have remembered.' And that was the truth — whatever he might think.

He gave a humourless laugh.

'How come? When you claim to have forgotten everything else? But as it happens, it doesn't matter because I know who you are.'

'What? How?'

He ignored her. 'And don't try telling me that Stephen didn't send you here.

6

That's obvious. What I can't quite work out is why? What's he up to?' He sat down on the bed, leaning towards her. 'I think you'd better come clean and tell me.'

'No. That's impossible. How could he?' She tried to shake her head but that hurt too much.

'Ah — but you know who Stephen is, don't you? That's miraculously come back to you.'

Cat sighed. It had been so tempting, but obviously this man knew too much, somehow. And there was no point in making her situation worse by inventing things.

She said, miserably, 'Yes. We're engaged.'

'Hmm. That's interesting.' He nodded, obviously thinking. 'And you've appeared here out of the blue, without knowing how you got here. Let's assume I'm going along with that, for now. What was the last thing you do remember?'

She dipped her head, trying to think. 'I was on my hen night.'

'Ah — you mean this may be one of

those typical hen night pranks? Although it's a stunt that more usually happens to the groom, I believe.'

She looked up, horror mixed with realisation.

'No — it can't have been. Amanda was organising it. She's my best friend. She knows she has to look after me. I can't drink, you see. I'm on permanent medication. It's a genetic condition but I'm fine as long as I don't drink. Amanda wouldn't have let me touch any alcohol . . .'

She faltered to a stop. She remembered having a jokey conversation with Amanda only a few days ago. She had said, 'If I drank, who knows where I might end up?'

He was saying, 'Although talking of the groom, maybe he had something to do with this?'

She shook her head.

'That doesn't make sense.'

'Does any of this make much sense? But if you can at least remember being out on your hen night, with any luck,

Cat, you will have remembered who you are.'

She stared at him. This was becoming more and more confusing.

'How do you know my name?'

'That's easy. I've seen photos of you on Stephen's phone. Perhaps he'd forgotten that. It was right at the beginning when he first met you. When he'd split up with the last one — Amanda, wasn't it? Presumably the Amanda you just mentioned.'

Playing for time, she said, 'Well, yes — but I don't see how you can remember me. Just from a picture on a phone.'

'Not hard, Cat. You're not easy to forget.' He was staring at her intently. She shivered, staring back into the green eyes. As if they were at the beginning of something life-changing.

His tone altered as he said suddenly, 'Ah, hang on. I think I get it.' His eyes were different now, alight with eagerness. 'He's found something out, hasn't he? He always said he'd let me know. I have to admit, knowing Stephen and after all this time, I'd just about given up on that. Seems a bit strange that he'd send you to tell me, but that way, I suppose no one would suspect any-thing. OK then, what does he want me to do? Where am I to go?'

Cat stared at him, blankly. She knew she was disappointing him in some way but she was unable to do anything about it.

'I'm sorry. I don't understand any of this.'

'No, come on. You have to know something. It's what I've been waiting for. Why else would you be here? He's given you a message for me, hasn't he? A message for Greg?'

She put her hands to her forehead, moving restlessly, aware that the blanket was scratching her legs. 'I don't remem-ber that happening. But there really is a lot about what happened before I got here that I don't remember.' She looked round the small, bare room. 'Where's my bag?'

10

'You didn't have one.'

'What? I'm sure I did. When I set off.' She bit her lip. 'From home. I think I remember getting ready. And I know I was wearing this pink dress. The bag has my purse in, and my cards — my medication — and my phone. Was I mugged?'

She supposed she must have been. And that would embroil her in all kinds of complications. She would have to report it and make a statement.

'I suppose I'll have to go to the police . . . '

'No!'

His vehemence shocked her. She jerked backwards.

'Oh — OK then, I won't. Best not. I don't think I had much in my bag anyway.'

'Sorry.' He laid a hand on her arm, surprisingly gentle after the violence of his response. 'I didn't mean to scare you. But it's not a good idea.'

She swallowed and then chose each word cautiously.

'In that case, can I stay here a bit longer? Until I feel better? I still feel quite dizzy. And perhaps I'll remember something useful after all. Perhaps there was a message and I've forgotten it.'

His brows were closing again. She didn't think she'd seen anyone else frown like that. She was gazing at him in fascination. He was saying, 'Is that what you've been told to say? Is that it?'

'Told?' Forget the eyebrows. She must concentrate. She had to convince him. 'No — I'm sure I haven't.'

Who would have told her? Did he mean Stephen?

He seemed to be ignoring her, thinking aloud.

'But what possible advantage could there be in that? For Stephen, or for any of us?' He was looking directly at her again. 'When is this wedding supposed to be?'

'Saturday.' How long was that from now? 'I don't even know when that is.'

'If you stay here, you'll miss it. Not what you want, I would think. Or what

Stephen wants. We'll have to get you back.'

'Oh. So I haven't missed it already?' There was a heavy feeling beneath her ribs. Missing the wedding would have solved everything . . . She added in a low voice, 'But I don't think it is what I actually want. I think I've changed my mind.'

'What?' He threw himself up off the bed, striding over to the window. 'You've got to be joking. OK, so you and Stephen are having personal problems, but what has that to do with me? Why should you — and Stephen too, presumably — involve me in any of this and on top of everything else? It doesn't make sense.'

'Stephen doesn't know I've changed my mind. Not yet. I've only just realised myself. And on top of what? Have you got a problem, too?' She had some vague idea of keeping him talking, delaying any discussion about her having to go back. She said brightly, 'Perhaps I can help?'

13

Amanda's phone rang. She glanced at the number. 'Yes?' She realised she was holding her breath, smiled at herself and let it go.

The voice at the other end sounded almost amused. 'Do you want to know where she is?'

'No. That wasn't the agreement.'

'Pity. I think you'll be impressed.'

Nearby a door was closing. Amanda hissed, 'I can't talk now. I'll just wait and see, thanks. As we agreed.' She ended the call.

'Stephen? Is that you?' She softened her voice. 'Have you heard anything?'

Stephen's face was gaunt with anxiety. He shook his head. 'I don't understand. Something must have happened to her. Something bad. She wouldn't stay away deliberately.' He slumped down onto the sofa, his head in his hands.

Amanda made her voice reassuring. 'It's still very soon. I'm sure she'll turn up.'

14

'Soon?' He shook his head. 'We should be getting married tomorrow. This doesn't feel right.' He muttered, almost to himself, 'But perhaps I should wait. I haven't had any ransom demands.'

'What? Ransom demands? Whatever are you talking about?' Amanda paused as if trying to work this out. 'Why should there be?'

'Well, you know. I don't mean that she's been kidnapped. Or I don't think I do. I meant as some kind of pre-wedding stunt.'

Amanda looked at him closely. 'You don't look as if you believe that. You look far too upset.'

'I don't know what to think. I can't think.'

Amanda sighed. 'Yes, I know. It is very worrying. But I'm sure she'll be fine. She's resourceful.'

'But what if she doesn't turn up at all?'

'I think that's highly unlikely, but if so, we'll just have to cancel everything.'

'What?' He looked around the room,

confused. 'That wasn't what I meant. But I suppose you're right. But she might still turn up, don't you think, tomorrow — in time for it? At the Registry Office?'

Just like Stephen. So unrealistic. Unable to accept what was staring him in the face.

'She would have to come back here first, to get changed. Tell you what, if she isn't here by mid-morning tomorrow, I'll cancel everything for you. I have all the details, since I helped Cat to arrange it all. It's lucky you wanted to keep it simple.'

He said, 'I wanted to make sure of everything. Since I'd already lost — ' He stopped suddenly.

'Water under the bridge,' Amanda said. 'I never blamed you.'

He was obviously hardly listening.

'None of that matters. I just want her back.'

'Don't worry. I'm sure everything will work out.' Amanda sat down beside him. She said softly, 'I should never

16

have broken it off, should I? You and I. I'm so sorry.'

* * *

Greg's phone rang, making Cat jump. He swore, snatching at his pocket.

'Mike? Sorry, can't talk now. I'm a bit tied up here — What?'

She could hear Mike clearly. He must be shouting. 'Greg, listen! You have to get out. Now.'

'Got you. Will do.' He didn't even seem surprised, ending the call. He seemed to be filled with a new energy and purpose.

'We're leaving. Come on.'

'Me as well? What's happening? Are we in danger?'

'Nothing I wasn't expecting. And of course you as well. I'm not leaving you on your own until I know what's going on and why you're here.'

He seized her wrist, pulling her up off the bed. She swayed but managed to keep her balance, even when he bent to

17

retrieve her shoes.

Now he was pulling her out of this cottage and into an identical building adjoining it. One storey, two rooms, the same small, square windows. Cat had a brief impression of a vast, clear blue sky and a spread of green-blue sea below before they were inside again. This was obviously where Greg lived, though it was almost as sparsely furnished as the one she had been sleeping in.

His voice was abrupt.

'You can't go anywhere like that. You'll be far too visible. And those shoes are a waste of time.'

Cat looked down at the short crumpled dress, and the matching pink heels in Greg's hand.

'They're new.' What was she talking about? As if that mattered now.

He snorted, contempt in his voice.

'Don't worry, we're not leaving them. Too much of a giveaway. The shoes are going in my backpack. Here, put these on over the dress.' He was passing her a pair of jeans and a sweater as he spoke.

'Don't worry, they're clean. Too big for you but they'll be OK with this belt. And you can have my spare trainers with two pairs of thick socks. That should do it. And hurry up.'

She did as she was told. Why argue? None of this was any different from the general confusion she had experienced since she first came round. He was filling his backpack with what must be the rest of his own possessions, with terse, lightning movements. He didn't seem to have much. In minutes, this cottage looked as unoccupied as the other one.

Without pausing to ask whether she was ready, he was pulling her arm again. No point telling him her makeshift footwear wasn't the easiest. Would she have been better barefoot? Maybe not.

There was a beaten path leading from the cottages but they left it almost at once, striking off onto the rough ground. Even through the soles of her borrowed trainers, she could feel the pebbles. Wiry plants were catching at her ankles. With scrunching her feet and half jogging,

19

half skipping, she seemed to be managing quite well. She mustn't slow him down when he was taking this so seriously. Though he didn't seem too appreciative of her efforts.

Did he really think there was some kind of threat? Now they had been running for several minutes, she began to think that this was ridiculous. There was no sign at all of any danger. Everything around them was quiet and peaceful.

He was half bent double as he moved, and she followed his lead in that. The land sloped gently and turning briefly, she realised that the cottages were no longer in sight. Yet still they were ploughing on. It was almost as if she had been plunged into a virtual reality adventure game. She couldn't contain the questions any longer.

'Who are we running from? Where are we going?'

He shook his head. 'Tell you later.'

Better than nothing, she supposed.

They had reached a steeply downward slope and were progressing crabwise.

Suddenly he motioned to her. 'Wait here.' He was crawling back, peering cautiously over the top. 'Get down.'

'Why, what is it?' Although she was doing it anyway. 'What can you see?'

'Quiet. Come on.' They were going downwards again, faster now.

OK, I wanted to stay with him. I've no grounds for complaint. Though she had envisaged staying blissfully in that peaceful room with the amazing views. Not this headlong, unexplained flight.

'Something's burning. What is it? Did you see?' She raised her nose, sniffing.

'Almost there.' His grip on her wrist was even tighter. They were half leaping, half sliding.

'Is it the people we're running from? Have they set fire to something? Greg, what is it?' In her frustration and anger, she was almost shouting.

'There's a log pile by the cottages. Could be that. Or maybe the grass if it's dry enough.'

Or even the cottages themselves? Cat shivered.

'But why? And who are they?'

'I don't know; a warning maybe. I'm not waiting to find out. Not when I have you to worry about.'

She said angrily, 'You don't have to worry about me. I can look after myself.'

He laughed suddenly. 'And you've made a great job of that so far, haven't you?'

Cat realised they were descending a large overhang. Abruptly the slope had become a cliff. He was pushing her and supporting her at the same time. If she hadn't been hampered by the bulky trainers, she would have made a much better attempt at this.

She was almost falling down the last few feet, landing on the sand of a small, hidden cove. It had only become visible during the last hurried minutes of their descent. A small boat waited at what appeared to be a makeshift, roughly constructed jetty. He was removing a tarpaulin, pulling her in after him, busying himself with ropes.

22

'You've got a boat,' she said stupidly, stating the obvious. Unsurprisingly, he didn't answer. Something occurred to her. 'Are we on an island?'

'Only during the higher tides and storms. You can walk along a sand bar to the beach and the pinewoods usually. Can you row?'

She offered cautiously, 'I have done. On boating lakes. But what about the motor?'

'Don't worry. There's fuel. But we need to be well out of earshot first.'

She didn't argue — but wouldn't the sound carry across the water anyway? As if he was reading her thoughts again, he explained, 'Or at least we need to put a substantial distance in between us. So that catching up with us by road will be almost impossible.'

She had more questions — plenty of them — but rowing took more effort than she had expected. She knew she was still affected by what had happened to her, and even with the exhilaration of their headlong flight and allowing for

23

her adrenalin kicking in, she still felt weaker than usual. It had been a while since she had taken her medication too — and it looked as though it might be a while longer until she was able to get a new supply.

Greg had been right. She wasn't able to look after herself. Not yet. She gritted her teeth, forcing herself on although the muscles in her arms were aching. With each stroke she felt as if she couldn't manage another, and yet she did.

When he said at last, 'That's it. You can stop now,' she felt as if she couldn't, that she had to keep going.

He put a gentle hand on her arm. 'Cat, stop.'

She looked up. They had rounded a headland. Were they nearing the main-land now? Oh, of course, it hadn't been a proper island anyway. She huddled down into an aching heap. Greg was stowing the oars, she realised dimly, and starting the motor. There was a welcome smell of fuel.

'First time,' she murmured. 'Lucky.'

'I've been ready for this. I check it every day.'

She took a weary breath. 'Prepared for what? And who were they? Did you see them?'

He said, 'Kind of.'

'How many were there?'

'Three.' He took his eyes briefly away from the sea ahead to give her a searching look. 'Don't try to tell me you don't know who they are.'

She was too tired to feel annoyed.

'I don't know.'

'Not Stephen, then?'

'No.' She paused. 'Not as far as I know. I told you, I don't know anything about any of this. Was Stephen there? Did you see him?'

'No.'

'Anyway, why should it be Stephen? You said it could be a warning.' The weary muscles in her arms were settling down to a dull ache. 'Do you mean he's threatening you? That doesn't sound much like him.'

She sighed, remembering how vulnerable Stephen could be. He was so prone to anxiety, always worrying. She had wanted only to help him. He would never be aggressive or threatening, she was certain of that.

'You don't know it's anything to do with him. You didn't even get a good look at them. You can't have done.'

Greg shrugged.

'What about that man who phoned you?' she persisted. 'Mike, wasn't it? Did he say it was something to do with Stephen?'

Greg paused, frowning again.

'You're right. He would have said if Stephen had been involved. OK, discussion over. I'd better concentrate on where we're going now.'

They continued in silence. Cat turned to look back. The land seemed an uncomfortable distance away. In all the other directions stretched nothing but empty sea. She was glad it was calm.

Was that a cloud of black smoke past

the headland, in the distance behind them? Perhaps the fire was taking hold even more, spreading through the dry vegetation. Other people must have noticed it.

Greg had mentioned a beach and pinewoods. If there were tourists there, some of them would have called the fire service by now. If she and Greg had stayed nearby, hidden, they could have waited for the firefighters to arrive. They would have been safe then.

But of course, the police would have been involved too — and he hadn't wanted the police.

None of this made much sense. Were they in real danger or not? She knew nothing about Greg. Could she believe anything he said? Or was this whole thing an invention — even though she desperately wanted to believe him?

She had a feeling that one way or the other, she would soon be finding out.

2

As they sped across the water, Cat could no longer stay awake. She only realised she must have dozed off when they jerked to a stop on yet another beach. Once again, at first she couldn't recall where she was and what she was doing.

Oh, yes, this was Greg, pulling her up and over the side, splashing through the shallow water. Everything was pushing and pulling, she thought.

Once more, she had to concentrate on keeping up, with her leg muscles aching. Up a sandy path, to feel a brief relief when they reached the top — but still they were moving onwards, in and out of close-growing pine trees, with another rough track beneath their feet instead of sand. It was almost dark now but Greg kept going.

Ahead, she saw the glint of something metallic among the pine needles.

Greg muttered something. He sounded pleased.

It was a vehicle. Cat could make it out at last. A battered old Land Rover. Cat could have wept with relief. She hadn't thought her legs would hold up much longer. But she had wanted this, hadn't she? She almost fell against it.

Greg said, almost kindly, 'It's OK now.'

Cat said, 'Is this where you keep it?'

How weak and pathetic her voice seemed.

He laughed. 'That wouldn't be too convenient. No, this is Mike again. He'll have left me the key. And some emergency rations, hopefully.'

Yes, Cat thought. *He's relieved too.*

Now, however, she had to get inside. The step up seemed huge. Her legs were shaking. She couldn't make them bend properly.

'Come on. It's OK.' Strong hands were around her waist, warm and firm. He had seen the problem and was giving her a hitch up.

The shabby leather seat was hard and

uncomfortable; it didn't matter. It was bliss just to sit down, without having to move her limbs. She chewed one of the energy bars he found in the glove compartment and then, as the Land Rover bounced along, she slept again. Until they stopped and she jerked forwards.

'Sorry. Brakes not too good. Here we are.'

Cat blinked, gazing around blearily.

'Oh. It's a shed. But it doesn't matter.'

'Don't worry. We can have a good night's sleep. Everything will seem clearer in the morning.'

'Yes, sorry. I do still need to sleep. I can't seem to wake up properly.'

'And then maybe we can get a few things sorted.' His voice was abruptly grim again.

She was too tired now to work out what he meant. Too tired even to make any kind of attempt at clambering out. Her head lolled against the back of the seat. Dimly she was aware of him opening her door.

It was a shed, though. How could

they possibly sleep in it? There wouldn't be room.

He half carried her inside. Bunk beds! That explained it. He was tipping her gently onto the bottom one. There was a thin, musty pillow and a rough blanket. Once more, she sank into the welcome darkness of sleep.

★　★　★

A hand was over her mouth. Another hand was roughly shaking her awake. This time, she was swiftly alert.

'Greg? What is it?' Her voice was muffled by the hand.

'Keep quiet.' An ominous hiss, next to her ear. 'You're coming with us.'

That wasn't Greg's voice. What did he mean? Who were these people? She was being pulled to her feet, yet again. Out of the door. Where was Greg? It was already light. She could see at once that the Land Rover had gone. Was this deliberate? Had she been wrong to trust him?

She couldn't see the two who were manhandling her, but round the side of the hut was parked a dark, modern SUV. A third man, leaning against the bonnet, was easily visible. He was smartly dressed in a dark suit with short dark hair, sleekly handsome and with an easy smile. He straightened as they stumbled towards him.

'Have you no finesse, you two? I'm sure Cat will be discreet if asked politely.'

Cat felt her knees sag with relief. It must be all right. They knew her name.

'Did Stephen send you?' she ventured.

He grinned. 'You could say that.'

'Where's Greg?'

He shrugged. 'Seems to have wandered off.'

No, he wouldn't do that. Would he? She was still trying to process all this as the smooth one assisted her into the SUV. Greg had thought they were safe here — and knew that she still needed to sleep, particularly after all the physical effort she had made.

The good-looking one threw the keys

to the person holding her. 'I can trust you to drive, I suppose? I'll look after our guest.'

You *fool*, she suddenly told herself. Yes, there were three of them. These were the three Greg had run from, after the phone call alerting him of the danger. The three who had set fire to the cottages. She should have realised straight away.

And yet they knew her name and seemed to have come from Stephen. Perhaps they had been sent to look for her? That would make sense.

But she couldn't approve of Stephen's choice. There had been no need for the rough treatment by the two who had woken her. Why would she object, if Stephen was behind this?

The good-looking one, now sitting next to her in the rear seats, seemed preferable. Much more civilised. And yet there was something about his smile that she didn't like.

She said cautiously, 'I don't understand.'

'You're not alone in that. However, don't worry — everything will soon be made clear, I would hope. And then we can deliver you safely to wherever you choose.' He paused. 'And whoever.'

Cat said, 'Thank you.' Since he was making a point of being polite, she might as well be equally polite in return. Except that inside, she felt like screaming. *Will somebody please just explain what's happening?*

Something occurred to her. Had Greg been telling the truth? Why had he been asking her all those questions when she didn't know the answers — instead of telling her what *he* knew?

But if he had, would she have understood any of it, considering the way she had been feeling when she first woke up? Just standing up had taken way too much effort. And her thoughts had been fully occupied with trying to work out what she could remember . . . and what she was going to do about Stephen.

Now however, she was in a different situation altogether. She had to gain all the information she needed from these three instead. If they could be persuaded to tell her anything. She would have to negotiate with them somehow.

The good-looking one was regarding her thoughtfully as if hoping to read her mind. He repeated, 'And to whoever you choose?' But this time, turning it into a question.

'I see. Have you come from Stephen? Did he arrange this?' She knew as she spoke that it didn't make sense. Why all the drama? Why not just turn up and say *Excuse me, our friend Stephen seems to have mislaid his bride. We've come to collect.* But then, that Mike or whoever he was, on the phone, hadn't given them the chance to do anything like that, she supposed. No wonder they seemed edgy.

'Well, you know how Stephen is. Always putting things off. We're independent. We arranged this ourselves. But on Stephen's behalf.' He gave her a confident smile. 'You know, I think it's time we introduced ourselves. My name is Dean Bryston. And these are my brothers.' He had pronounced the name slowly, with deliberation. 'Does that mean anything to you?'

'No, I don't think so. Have I met you?'

'That's disappointing. I thought you might have heard of us.'

She looked into the pale blue eyes. Had she seen him before? She shook her head.

'I don't think so. And it's quite an unusual name. I think I would have remembered if I had.'

'That's a shame.'

The SUV jolted over something on the path; it felt like a large rock.

'Sorry about that. This track's a bit uneven.' Dean Bryston put an arm round her shoulders.

Cat tensed, wanting to move away but they were immediately jolted even closer.

'Don't worry about my arm. Merely for safety purposes.'

Cat could see the driver's eyes in the

mirror. He half-turned, grinning. Obviously he was driving in this way deliberately, seeking out the worst parts of the track. The man in the passenger seat turned to face her, laughing.

'Now then,' her companion said. 'Gently now, Jimmy. You're frightening the lady. And we wouldn't want that now, would we?'

The passenger said, 'Oh, I don't know. Could be useful.'

'Shut it, Charlie,' his brother snapped suddenly, making her jump. His grip around her shoulders tightened. 'There's no need for it. Yes, of course we want Cat to tell us everything we need to know before we deliver her. But everything will be happening in a civilised fashion.'

What did he mean? What did they need to know? But she must not give him the slightest inkling that she had no idea what he was talking about. At least not until she had to.

She said, 'I'll be happy to help you, if I can.'

'That's good.' He relaxed a little.

'That's very good indeed. Excellent.'

Cat was thinking furiously. What could they possibly want? Could they be after her bank account details? She and Stephen had been saving for a house deposit. At the moment, they were sharing a rented flat. Her flat; Stephen had moved in with her.

Though he was often so busy at work that he wasn't there all that often. And the amount in her savings account was pitifully small.

It wouldn't be worth all this effort for three people. Besides, even if they took her to the nearest bank branch, she couldn't do anything since she didn't have her bag and her cards.

And that was stupid as it couldn't be anything they wanted from her. It must be something else entirely — as where did Greg come into it? Keep calm. Wait and see.

Her companion said, 'This will do.' They came to a stop. He took her arm and bundled her out — not aggressively, but his grip was tighter than necessary. The other two jumped out too, slamming their doors.

'No need for you two now,' Dean said. 'I can handle this. I know Cat is going to be reasonable.'

'I'm sure she is,' the one called Charlie smirked. 'But a bit of assistance never comes amiss.'

'And I'm not being left out of it,' Jimmy snarled.

Dean sighed. 'See what I have to put up with, Cat. I get the feeling they don't trust me. So be it. Let's get on with it. Down this track, here.'

'What for?' Charlie protested. 'We're wasting time with all this.'

'Leave it to me, will you?'

They were all walking quickly, slightly downhill, Cat and her partner in front and the other two behind. The trees thinned and they were suddenly standing at the top of a cliff, with nothing but a wide expanse of sea before them.

Cat gasped. She'd assumed, all that time she had been driven in the two

vehicles, first with Greg and then with
these three, that they were travelling
inland. Instead, they must have been
making their way along the coast.

'Beautiful, isn't it?' Dean said,
conversationally.

'Yes. It is.'

He twisted her arm around her back
a little. Any further and the movement
would have been painful. Cat said
nothing.

He said, in the same easy tone, 'It's a
long way down.'

Cat's heart was thudding. She said,
'Yes.'

'Right. The thing is, Cat, who has the
money — and where is it?'

3

'Money?' Cat's mouth was dry. 'I don't know what you mean. What money?'

Dean shook his head. 'Now, then. I'm afraid that isn't what we wanted to hear. Not at all.'

Jimmy muttered, 'I knew this would be a waste of time. Just shove her over and forget it.'

Cat pressed her lips together, trying not to react but suspecting that the blood had drained from her face. If they were hoping to scare her half to death, they were succeeding.

'And how would that help?' Dean said. 'We would lose our advantage. Whoever has the money might be eager to make an exchange.'

Charlie said, 'We could get rid of her anyway and pretend we still had her. They wouldn't know. Would save us a lot of time and trouble. She's just a liability, if you ask me.'

Dean smiled. 'I didn't ask you — but I suppose it's an idea. Do you hear that, Cat?' He nudged her forward and her feet slid a little. She gasped. 'But there again, you may well have the information we need. The thing is — we think one of your boyfriends has our money. And naturally we want it back. We're not suggesting that you're implicated in this, darling, but it would help if you told us which one has it. That might just be enough to satisfy us.'

He must mean Greg or Stephen. Although why would they think Greg was her boyfriend? She'd only just met him. And how would she know whether he had this money or not? He didn't give that impression.

Neither did Stephen. He never seemed to have any money — or she had assumed he hadn't, because he was living with her without contributing to the rent.

Not that she would have dreamed of asking him. Not at that time, when he had been so vulnerable and upset and needed a refuge. When they had first got together Cat had just had an overwhelming urge to protect him. She had felt so sorry for him when he was on the rebound from Amanda.

Still, that hadn't been enough. She could see that now. She had never loved him — not properly. The whole thing was such a mess.

'I'm a patient man, Cat. Not like my brothers. I'm afraid they can get very short-tempered if they have to wait too long for anything. So I think we need an answer now.' Dean Bryston's voice was filled with menace.

She took a deep breath, trying to speak calmly.

'If you mean Stephen or Greg, neither of them has said anything to me about this money. I'm really sorry if it's yours and if I knew anything I'd tell you, of course I would.'

'Just like I said,' Charlie grumbled. 'Get rid of her, end of.'

'Please, no!' Cat glanced down and

43

wished she hadn't. The height of the cliff was making her head swim. 'Perhaps I can help you.'

'Oh, yes? And how would that work?'

'As I said, I don't know the answer to your question. But I'm sure I could find out for you. Let me go and I can ask where the money is.'

Dean demanded sharply, 'Ask who?'

'Either of them. Both of them.'

Charlie hooted with laughter.

'You're not falling for that, bro?'

Dean was pausing, head on one side, almost in a theatrical gesture. He let go of her arm and she sensed that he was taking a step back. Her heart leaped. Was he going along with her suggestion?

'Hey, bro?'

There was contempt in Charlie's voice.

'No, of course I'm not. Somewhat unfortunately for you, Cat. You could tell us anything, leaving us here while you carry out this alleged quest but doing nothing to help us at all. You

44

could just carry on with whatever you wanted to do. As you were. Having told one or both of these boyfriends of yours what we want — and all about us.'

Cat opened her mouth to deny it — but knew she couldn't. Not with any conviction. It was all too obvious that he was right. She hesitated.

Dean laughed, clearly enjoying her discomfort.

Jimmy muttered, 'Like we said. Get rid of her. Shove her over.'

As he spoke, there was an explosion from the trees behind them. The three men spun round. For one moment they were all frozen in shock before Dean shouted something indistinct and turned to run in the direction of the noise.

Cat could hear other smaller explosions and the crackle of flames. Could it be the SUV? Again Dean shouted over one shoulder as he ran; he might have said, 'Get her,' although again the words were unclear. The other two were already following, however, taking no notice.

Cat didn't wait for them to realise

their mistake. She was off, running along the top of the cliff, away from the track they had followed — as far as she could tell. With the sea on her left, maybe she was heading north? Any direction, she didn't care, as long as it was away from where she could still hear the vehicle burning, like a collection of fireworks. How long would it take for the worst of the fire to be over, for things to quieten down, for the three to realise there was nothing they could do? And then they would remember her and come looking.

She continued stumbling straight ahead in Greg's oversized trainers — but where to? The way they had come, they had seemed to drive her through the pine forest for miles. It might extend for miles in this direction too, for all she knew. She was stumbling over tree roots, gorse catching at her borrowed sweater.

This was hopeless. Would it be better to hide and hope they would give up and go away?

No, far better to keep going. They

wouldn't give up — and where was there to hide here? Even the gorse bushes were scrubby and sparse, and she doubted whether she could have crawled inside one without scratching herself to pieces.

It was no good, she had to stop. There was a stitch in her side and her breath was coming in great panting gasps. Just for five minutes. Could she still hear the fire? She rested one hand against the rough bark of the nearest pine tree.

Abruptly there was a hand over her mouth. Her eyes widened in horror.

Someone hissed, 'Sshhh — don't scream. You'll give us away.'

She recognised the voice and sighed in relief.

'I wasn't going to.' Yes, she would have done. But she wasn't going to admit that.

'It's me,' Greg said. And briefly, so briefly she almost wondered if she was imagining it, his lips were on hers, in a kiss that was over almost before it had begun.

Cat could hardly speak. Her lips were burning. Her emotions were in turmoil. She managed to say, 'I get that. What took you so long?'

'Never mind. This way. Quietly. It's not far.'

'What isn't far?'

'The Land Rover.'

She saved the remainder of her breath for following at a limping jog, as fast as she could manage. Greg was right — here it was. Refuge.

She clambered up, pleased at managing the step without help this time. Just as well, as Greg was already in the driving seat and starting up. She closed the heavy door as quietly as she could, wincing at the inevitable slam and at the roar of the engine.

'Sorry. That can't be helped,' Greg said. 'It's feeling its age. I'm hoping they're too far away to hear. Very fortunate you ran in the right direction. That's given us an advantage.'

He handed her a bottle of water and she drank gratefully. She wound the stiff window down a little.

'I can hear them shouting.'

'It's OK now we've got going. They've no chance of catching us. Not on foot.'

'Are you sure?' They hadn't seemed the kind to give up easily. 'Supposing they radio ahead and get those spikes put across in front of us?'

He laughed. 'They're not the police, Cat. I shouldn't think they have those resources.'

'So who are they, then? You have to tell me — I need to know what's going on.' She glanced sideways, looking at him properly for the first time. 'You're hurt! There's blood on your head. What happened?'

'I'm fine. Not as bad as it looks. I thought I heard something when you were asleep. Stupidly, I drove along the track to investigate and got out when I came to a log across the track. Schoolboy error — I should have known better.'

'I should think they're more used to this kind of thing than either of us.'

'They slipped up, though.' He grinned

at her. 'They should have hit me harder.'

She shivered. 'They will next time. After what you did to that vehicle. It looked very expensive.'

He said easily, 'They'll have insurance.'

'And you didn't answer my question. Who are they? They said they were called Bryston and I should know the name. But I don't.'

'Yeah. OK, of course I'll tell you. But let's park up somewhere safe first. I need to concentrate on driving this thing; it isn't the easiest.' He smiled grimly. 'Not like theirs would have been.'

Was he making excuses to avoid telling her? Cat wasn't sure. And she wasn't entirely convinced those three wouldn't get hold of someone or other on the phone, and get them to come and cut them off. It would only take another fallen tree blocking the way and they would be trapped!

They took a sharp right turn, along what was hardly a track at all. No doubt it was the wisest course of action but

Cat felt as if every bone in her body was being jolted.

Greg stopped and Cat glanced round. They were still amongst the trees. Surely they hadn't come far enough? Greg took out his phone.

'Mike? Hasn't worked as we'd hoped, mate. I need you to do something else for me. Remember Plan B? Now's the time.'

Why must he always be so cryptic? Didn't he trust her? She sighed. Probably not. Or did he think his phone might be hacked and someone could be listening in? No — she was being ridiculous now, allowing a fevered imagination to run away with her. But after everything that had happened, could anyone blame her?

There was no time to think this through because they were off again. More rattling and shaking before at last they shot out of the trees and onto a narrow lane; Tarmac and civilisation.

Greg showed no sign of stopping, however. The nightmare drive seemed to go on for hours. She could no longer complain that he wasn't putting enough distance between them and their pursuers. He was driving far too fast for the age of the vehicle and the condition of the roads, only slowing when they encountered buildings or pedestrians.

The first time it happened, Cat queried it.

'Are we there?'

'If we go too fast, we look conspicuous. People could be annoyed and remember us.'

She nodded, hanging onto the seat and the door handle and closing her eyes. But when they stopped again, there was no sign of anyone apart from a man standing by an old Ford Focus. It was almost as rusty and dented as the Land Rover; any more battered and that would have been conspicuous in itself.

Greg said, 'Change of transport. Come on.'

Cat needed no encouragement to leave the Land Rover. Perhaps she was being ungrateful when she had been so pleased to see it to begin with. But enough was enough.

This must be Mike. Tall, dark, bearded, in green canvas trousers and camouflage-type jacket. She couldn't see his face properly.

Greg was clapping Mike on the shoulder.

'Thanks, mate. I owe you one for all this.'

Mike laughed. 'Too right. I'll hold you to that.' What did he mean? But Greg wasn't querying the remark. Mike went on, 'Keys, here. There's cash in the dash. Where are you heading?'

Greg shrugged. 'Best to keep moving for now. I'll let you know when we get there.'

'Well — suppose. Just wanted to be ready if you needed more help.'

'Thanks,' Greg said. 'I'm hoping we won't.'

Mike shook his head.

'Do you actually have any kind of plan? Or are you just winging it, as usual?'

'Something will come to me.' Greg gestured to Cat and she slid into the passenger seat.

'Those people — if they're who I think they are — it's not good to get on the wrong side of them.'

Greg gave him another of those careless grins.

'Too late for that. I suspect I'm there already — on their wrong side.'

'And what are you going to do about her?'

'Sorry — got to go. Speak later.'

Cat turned as they drove off. Mike was staring after them. A hand obscured his face as he waved; he hadn't sounded too happy, Cat thought. Maybe he was worried about them. She couldn't blame him.

She asked, 'Yes, what are you going to do about me?'

'Don't worry. That's something else we need to discuss. But before we talk, we must do something about the way we look.'

'I see that,' she said slowly. No point

in changing the car if they both looked just the same. 'How do you mean? Cutting our hair? Dyeing it?'

He laughed. 'Some less conspicuous clothes will do for starters. Particularly for you.'

'I'll go with that. I must look ridiculous. Not that I mind,' she added hastily. 'It was necessary at the time, I can see that.'

'We need a town with several charity shops, where we're less likely to look obvious. Get a couple of things you need in each. And we'll go separately. That way no one will remember us.'

'Unless charity shops have CCTV.' She had meant that as a joke, trying to lighten the mood.

'We'll have to hope not.'

'I didn't mean that seriously. Those three won't be able to check CCTV footage, will they?'

'No, of course not.'

But the police could. And he hadn't wanted her to go to the police, had he? A shudder snaked across her shoulders.

55

Don't be stupid, she told herself. *I'm not in any trouble with the police. Avoid the Brystons and everything will be fine.*

And in spite of everything, she wanted to stay with Greg. It seemed that she could be useful to him somehow — as well as to the other three.

They had at last arrived in a small town. There was a small street market along the main street. Even better. She sought out the charity shops as Greg had suggested and bought jeans, a couple of tops, trainers that fitted and a large patchwork bag for the spares and her borrowed clothes. She purchased new underwear from the street market, and a waterproof jacket. An odds and ends stall for a scrunchy to tie her hair back. Once she had everything she needed, she changed in the public toilets.

Greg nodded his approval. He'd ditched his nature warden look for a dark tracksuit top and jeans. He said,

'There's a supermarket just out of the town. We can park up, buy some food and then talk in the car park. No one will notice us.'

He was right. The blue Focus merged into the rows of other cars. The shoppers, mainly parents with children or elderly couples, were all concentrating on manoeuvring their shopping trolleys and loading up their car boots.

Devouring the last of her sandwich, Cat turned to him.

'So what is all this about? Why are we going to so much trouble? What did those brothers want and why are we avoiding the police?'

Greg stared straight ahead, avoiding her gaze.

'I've been accused of murder.'

4

'What?' Cat stared at him, feeling as if all the blood was draining from her face. 'Did you say murder?'

No wonder he had been reacting so oddly at times. He needed to hide. He was on the run.

Greg's knuckles were white as he gripped the steering wheel. 'Accused wrongly. I didn't do it.'

So there had been some kind of a mistake. Of course there had been.

'Were you arrested? Questioned? How are you here? Did you escape?' She was trying to sound cool and calm but the words were pouring out of her. 'No wonder you didn't want to take me to the police.'

He was still avoiding looking at her directly.

'No. But to answer your understand-able questions, I wasn't arrested. I

58

wasn't even questioned. We didn't let it get that far. I ran.'

She said blankly, 'Oh. I see.' But of course, she didn't. Tentatively, she added, 'Was that a good idea?'

'Not as it's turned out. It was a huge mistake.'

That unwanted thought was wriggling its way into her head again. Was Greg telling the truth? And if not, was she in danger? Out of the frying pan, into the fire. Was she any safer with Greg than she had been with the three mysterious brothers? Best not to antagonise him. To be on the safe side.

She nodded. 'Well — I think I can understand it. You see all those TV documentaries, don't you, where devastating mistakes have been made and the wrong person entirely serves a long prison sentence.'

'Sometimes.'

There were so many questions she needed to ask. She hardly knew where to start.

'Wait a minute — you said 'we'. As in

'We didn't let it get that far'. Who else was involved?'

She had a feeling that she already knew.

'You know, don't you? You already know about this?' He was looking at her now.

Cat answered carefully.

'No, of course not. I mean, I don't know. I think I may have guessed.' She sighed. 'I don't know anything. Like I told you from the beginning.'

He shrugged. 'OK. I'll have to go along with that for now.'

And there was the biggest question of all. Her mouth was feeling dry. 'Who was murdered?'

Greg was looking resigned.

'Yes, OK. I'll start at the beginning.' He was tapping his fingers on the dashboard, as if ordering his thoughts. 'I've been over this again and again. Years ago, when we left uni, three of us went into business together. Briefly, it involved contacts and apps to provide business opportunities and finance for

60

unknown entrepreneurs. Fairly innovative at the time. Stephen and I, and Vincent. We were all mates, we worked well as a team. Each of us with different abilities — online, products, sales, finance — but we all gelled together, bouncing ideas off each other.'

'And?' she encouraged.

'We began by working from our homes which worked well, since we were all based in the North West. We all had a rough idea of what the others were doing — or I thought we did. Vincent was a whizz with finance. Stephen and I trusted him. Why wouldn't we? We seemed to be doing OK. More than OK. Much more. What had begun as a small, basic idea had gained the potential to become huge.'

'It doesn't sound too different from what Stephen does now. But he doesn't work on his own. He's employed.'

'Yes.' Greg took a breath. 'There's no way round this next part. I only wish there was. Stephen and I were talking about expanding; an inevitable next step. Getting premises, taking people on. Vincent didn't seem that keen. He said he didn't think we were ready for that. Give it another year or so, he said, and we would be more secure. That would be the time for expansion. I thought he was being over-cautious. But whatever, we left it.'

Greg closed his eyes.

'Then it all began to fall apart. Stephen came to me and told me he thought Vincent was fiddling the accounts. Stephen had managed to have a look at them and some things didn't make sense. Stephen thought we were making more than Vincent was letting on. I didn't believe it. There must have been a misunderstanding — Stephen must have got it wrong. And anyway, we had to give Vincent a chance to explain. So Stephen and I arranged to go round to see him.' He paused.

Cat was holding her breath. She didn't want him to stop because she sensed he was coming to the whole point of what had happened. She mustn't do anything to interrupt him, in case he changed his mind about telling her.

Greg leaned back, resting his head against the seat rest. 'I got there first. Vincent had a flat in a refurbed warehouse in Manchester. I knew something was wrong straight away, because his door was part open. He wouldn't have left it like that. He was very security conscious. I called his name but there was no answer so I went in.'

'And what happened?' Cat was almost whispering.

'The sitting room door was open too, so I could see straight through. There was an empty space on the table where he always used his laptop. And Vincent was lying on the floor with blood on his head — and his hands. Blood everywhere. I didn't get it at first. I didn't realise he was dead. I had some mad idea of doing first aid, making a tourniquet to stop the bleeding, exerting pressure. I threw myself down on my knees next to him. I thought I could help him. It all gets a bit blurred then but I felt this heavy blow to my head. I don't think I was out very long but when I came round, trying to pull myself up — suddenly Stephen was there too, standing over me, looking down.'

'Stephen?' Of course, in the horror of the narrative, Cat had forgotten he was supposed to be part of this as well. Her throat tightened. 'Did he hit you?'

Greg said, with a bitter resignation, 'I don't think so. And I'll never forget the look on his face. He was horrified and disgusted. He said, 'Greg, what have you done?' I'll never forget it.'

Cat said indignantly, 'But you hadn't!' She bit her lip. Or not if Greg was telling her the truth. She only had his word for it. But he seemed so convincing. She wanted to believe him.

'Stephen thought I had. Or so he said.'

Cat brushed her hand across her eyes. 'But he's never told me anything about any of this.' She had to admit,

64

however, that would be like Stephen. Pushing aside any unpleasantness and refusing to face up to the reality of it. Wanting to move on — into his new life with his new bride.

Greg was still speaking. 'I think I said, 'Who would have done this? Is it a burglary that's gone wrong? Have they taken anything?' And Stephen wasn't listening; he was talking over me and saying I hadn't to worry, he wouldn't betray a mate whatever I'd done. 'Just get out of here, Greg, and I'll tell the police it must have been a burglary gone wrong.''

'It sounds as if he didn't have any trouble hearing that last bit,' Cat said. She was feeling uneasy about Stephen's reaction. 'But, Greg, if you were innocent, wouldn't it have been better for you to explain the truth to the police? You only had to tell them what you've told me. And surely forensics would have proved your account.'

Greg groaned. 'Do you think I haven't gone over that? Over and over again. Sometimes I wish I'd ignored him and sometimes I think Stephen was right and it looked so bad that no amount of forensics would have cleared me. I had his blood on me.' He was tapping the steering wheel again. 'But I do remember telling him he had to believe me — I didn't do it. And Stephen said, 'OK, but just go.' He said, 'I'll sort everything — and when it's all been investigated and they've found who has done it, then you'll be able to come back.' He said I hadn't to worry, he was sure it wouldn't take long. If I stayed at the crime scene, it would just complicate matters.' He banged his fist onto the wheel. 'The most stupid decision I ever made.'

'Well, yes. I suppose what Stephen was saying sounded plausible. In a way.' She knew herself how convincing Stephen could be when he chose.

'I was in shock. All I could think of was, where could I go? And that I'd better get my passport.

'Stephen said, 'Wash your hands first.

You're covered in blood.' I said yes, he was right and I'd better go home and get some clean clothes. Stephen had been shocked too at first, but now he seemed almost calm. He said he would stay there and call the police when I'd had time to get well away.

'And suddenly my head cleared and I didn't know why, but I knew I wasn't going to ask any more of Stephen. I said, 'OK, you do that. But I can't involve you any further. I'll get hold of Mike.' I thought he was going to argue but he nodded and then he said, 'Good idea. But don't tell me what you decide to do. I'm better not knowing.' I said, 'But when it's all sorted you need to tell me.' He said, 'No problem. I've got Mike's number.''

There was another silence.

Cat prompted, 'And what happened then?'

'Nothing. That's how we left it. Weeks ago now. I've heard nothing and neither has Mike. That's why, when I recognised you, I assumed Stephen had sent you.' The green eyes were meeting hers again. 'You're certain he didn't?'

'No! I'm sure he can't have done. This is dreadful. I mean, I know I still don't know how I got here but even before that, Stephen never told me about any of this. I didn't even know anything about the business you shared together. You know Stephen and how he always talks a lot. Surely he would have said something? It's hard to imagine he would have been hiding it from me.'

'Is it?'

'Well — I suppose, although he talks a lot, it's almost always about himself. And during that very intense time when we first got together, he was talking about how he was feeling and how lost he was without Amanda — until we began to fall in love.' Cat hesitated. 'Or I thought we were. And he didn't say much more about her then.' But he had still said a great deal about how he was feeling and how lucky he was to have someone like me and how he couldn't possibly imagine ever being without me. 'Never leave me, Cat. I don't know what I would do.' She shifted uneasily. She was being horrible now, trying to justify what she knew she had to do. This wasn't helping Greg. Get back to the point.

She said briskly, 'He seems to have been very decisive on the spur of the moment. When he was faced with that terrible thing. Although I suppose he can be sometimes.'

'It sounds as if you got together pretty quickly.'

'Yes. I felt so sorry for him when Amanda dumped him. She was my best friend. Long term.'

'Yes, you mentioned that.'

She said hurriedly, 'I know what you're thinking. I shouldn't have gone out with my best friend's ex, even though she didn't want him for herself any more. It doesn't seem — well, sort of ethical somehow. But I asked Amanda whether she minded and she said she didn't.' Cat could remember exactly what Amanda had said because

69

it had troubled her at the time.

No, I don't mind at all. In fact I'm relieved. I knew suddenly that I couldn't do this. That I had to finish it. If you go out with him, perhaps it will cheer him up and stop me feeling so guilty. I hate seeing him so miserable. This will be the answer to everything.

And then we had a whirlwind romance, Cat thought. You bet. How foolish she had been. Her memory was working overtime now.

'Before we got together, I had a short term contract in Germany. Amanda was bringing Stephen over to meet me, at last. But it was nothing like I expected. Amanda seemed restless and preoccupied. And the next morning, she dumped Stephen, without warning. She said, 'I can't deal with this, Cat. I'm sorry. Help me out. He'll want a sympathetic ear. You were always a soft touch. You'll be ideal.' And she laughed — and flew home.

'And she was right. I was ideal. But he wanted more than a shoulder to cry on. It had seemed like love at the time — and Stephen had so obviously wanted it to be . . . ' Her voice trailed off.

Greg seemed to be dismissing this part of it.

'OK, so you were in Europe — but didn't you see any of what was happening here on the news? Or didn't Stephen ever think to mention it?'

'No, of course he didn't. We didn't bother watching TV. And it never occurred to me to catch up with the news online. Why should it? I was so caught up with getting to know him and falling in love. As I thought.'

'That's what I've been short of,' Greg muttered. 'Information. I've been relying on Mike but the reception where I was tended to be patchy. And Mike kept telling me he hadn't heard anything on the media. It was enough just to sit tight to begin with. No news was good news, as I thought — since no one seemed to be looking for me.'

'What were you actually doing there?

On the island?' She was curious suddenly. He hadn't seemed purpose-less. She hadn't got the impression that he was just hanging around.

'I was acting as a temporary nature and wildlife warden. On Mike's behalf. He's responsible for various endangered sites and species, though he isn't employed by any of the big charities. That island belongs to his parents.'

She said wistfully, 'It seemed idyllic.'

'Yes. In other circumstances, it would have been. A huge change from the machinations and pressures of the rat race. When all this is over, it could be something I'd like to go back to. But we were talking about Stephen . . .'

'Yes. Sorry.' Cat bowed her head, picking at the stretchy fabric of her leggings. 'Getting married was his idea, of course.'

'Oh, of course.'

She ignored his sarcasm. 'I know. But I thought after having his heart broken, he wanted security. It was all so fast.' She stared out of the window, to where a small, uneven hedge marked the edge of the car park. 'I know now that I've made a terrible mistake.'

Greg's voice was almost harsh.

'So what are you going to do?'

'I thought — ' Cat hesitated. 'You seemed to be telling me I could be useful to you. Isn't that why I'm here? Can I stay?'

'No. You can't. I've changed my mind.'

'Oh.' She felt the heat of anger and then a chill, feeling unexpectedly bereft. 'I've convinced you I don't have any kind of message and know nothing, and so I'm of no further use? Is that it?'

It was ridiculous to feel like this. She hardly knew him. In a different world, however, she could have been deeply attracted to him. She had never felt this way about Stephen. How could she have ever imagined that she loved him?

Snap out of it, Cat, she told herself. She was as bad as Stephen, feeling sorry for herself. And none of this was helping.

'No — not at all. Far from it.' He put his hand on her arm, his touch almost gentle. 'You mustn't think that. It's because I see now that by keeping you here with me, I'm putting you into an unacceptable measure of danger. And I'm not prepared to do that.'

'From the Bryston brothers? But we've lost them. They can have no idea where we're going. And they didn't hurt me.'

He looked at her carefully. 'I didn't have time to ask you about that. Are you sure?'

She tried to get as near to the truth as she dared. 'They were trying to threaten me a bit but it wasn't convincing.' She crossed her fingers. 'They were very polite about it. Or one of them was — the one who did most of the talking.'

Don't mention that they had wanted to throw me off the cliff. Greg would have me back home in the blink of an eye.

Greg was shaking his head.

'Only because it wasn't in their interest to hurt you. Not at that time. But if they managed to catch up with you again, they might well threaten you, to get at me.'

That was uncomfortably close to what had happened.

'We'll just have to make sure that they don't. I'm not running away — that makes it look as if they've won.'

'It's not worth the risk.'

Better to change the subject slightly, although she still wasn't quite ready to reveal everything the brothers had said. She wasn't sure why.

'Who were they, anyway? They seemed to think I should have heard of them. But the name doesn't mean anything to me.'

'Vincent who died. Our partner. They're his brothers.'

'Oh. I see.'

That made them even more dangerous, didn't it? They had been asking about money, but presumably they would be after revenge as well. Cat tried to suppress a shudder. She pushed on.

'But you do need me. You can't manage those three on your own.'

She couldn't quite envisage what she could possibly do but surely between them, they could think of something? Something proactive.

Greg said, 'If you really want to help me — '

'Yes, I do. Of course I do.'

'Good. Then you can go back to Stephen and see what you can find out. I need to know what he knows. His version of what happened.' He was looking at her with a thoughtful gaze. 'I think he's more likely to tell you than anyone else.'

'Oh.' This wasn't what Cat had wanted at all. 'Well, yes. I do have to see him again — and I need my medication from the flat. But I don't intend on staying long. I just need to tell him I can't marry him after all.'

'I'm sorry,' Greg said quietly. 'I would rather not ask when you're in this difficult situation. But I need to know.'

Bad enough to be breaking this news to Stephen as it was. And now this.

'I don't quite see what you mean. Unless you think Stephen has found something out but hasn't told you.'

'Yes, maybe. I can't understand why I haven't heard anything from him. He's always been very focussed when he sets his mind to a project. I don't see why this should be any different.'

'Yes, that's true.'

Stephen had definitely been very focussed in his pursuit of her, Cat thought.

'I was beginning to think something must have happened to him. Looking into a murder can be a risky undertaking. Perhaps I shouldn't have expected it of him. But I know from you that he's fine, so it isn't that. He must have come up with some ideas about Vincent's death by now.'

'Perhaps he was waiting until he understood the whole thing?' As she spoke, Cat knew how feeble that sounded.

'Yes, I've considered that. And he and I both knew there were darker aspects to the way Vincent was running things. Who knows who Vincent might have been mixed up with, particularly when you consider what his brothers are like? But why wait? Stephen and I have been mates for a long time. He must know what I'm going through. He could have got a message to me through Mike, if nothing else.' He nodded decisively. 'No, I'd already decided before you showed up so unexpectedly, that I'd had enough of waiting. I'm going to sort things out myself.' He smiled. 'And then you arrived. Like a gift from heaven.'

Not quite in the way she would have liked him to mean that, Cat thought. Never mind. 'And now yes, I'm sure I can be useful to you in that.' Cat tried to sound positive. 'Obviously Stephen is the best place to start. And maybe I'll have to say nothing about leaving him.

Just to get him to open up to me?'

He took her hand. 'It's a big ask, I know. Except — I'm wondering about the combination of the meds and the alcohol and the physical and mental shock of what you've experienced. Could all that have caused you to act out of character? This decision to ditch Stephen might be a temporary thing.'

'Oh, no. No.' Cat shook her head. 'I feel completely clear-headed now. And thinking back, I can see I had doubts for a while. I'd just been suppressing them. And when — ' She stopped. 'No, it doesn't matter.' She had been about to tell Greg that his kiss had been the final proof that she had made the right decision. She blushed.

Greg was staring at her, a questioning look on his face. 'No? OK then, there's a lot you're free to tell him — about what you remember. Where you woke up, about meeting me and how I recognised you and told you what had happened. All of that.'

'Yes.' There was so much to go

through with Stephen without the bad news. She added, 'But I won't tell him where you are now. Just in case Stephen — well, just in case.'

Greg said, 'You won't know where I will be.'

'Oh. I see.' Her heart sank. Did that mean he still didn't trust her? Because he thought she was still influenced unduly by what had happened to her and her first loyalties would be to Stephen? She sighed. After all, why should he trust her? Everything she had told him was true, but it must have seemed barely convincing. No, he was right. This did make sense. *What I don't know can't be revealed to anyone.*

'I expect that's for the best.'

His voice was gentle. 'You're looking confused. Perhaps I am asking too much of you.' He moved a strand of her hair away from her face. 'I do think this will be the best way forward if we can pull it off. But I wonder if you're agreeing to everything I suggest far too easily? I haven't given you time to think it through. Whereas I've done nothing but think for the last few weeks.'

'It is what I want to do. I'll help you out now and think about things in more depth later, if you like.' She wished he would carry on stroking her hair, but he dropped his hand. Probably he had hardly been aware that he was doing it. She added, 'But I'll be lying to Stephen. I think that will make me seem awkward and he'll know I'm holding something back. He could even think it was something to do with you and Vincent.'

Greg nodded. 'That's very perceptive. You're right. Actually, yes, tell him about your change of heart. Say whatever you need to say. Be completely straight with him. But amongst all that, please ask him what he's found out.'

She smiled at him, relieved. 'I will. But if I don't know where you are, how am I to contact you? When I do have something to tell you?'

81

'I got two cheap pay-as-you-go phones when I was shopping. Untraceable. We'll have one each. Only phone me when you can't be overheard — and keep it as brief as possible.'

Happiness surged inside her. He had made these plans already, to keep in touch with her. He was looking into her eyes again, his gaze intense.

'Thanks. You don't know grateful I am.'

Cat was starting to say 'That's OK — ' when suddenly, he leaned forward and his lips were on hers. Yes! She had been right all along. This was what she wanted. She responded eagerly.

He moved away first, smiling.

'Sorry. Again. That seals our deal, OK?'

Cat gulped. Was that all it had been, for him?

She said softly, 'OK.'

5

As if nothing had changed, Greg found a taxi for her and pressed some notes into her hand. 'You'll need this for the fare. And it's best if I keep out of the way now.'

'What?' She looked up at him, her face blank. What did he mean? Was that it? Would she ever see him again? Once she had passed over whatever she found out, via the phone he'd given her, would that be the end?

'I'll leave you to it.'

'I see. OK, then.' *Be sensible, Cat.*

Did she want to see him again? Had this just been a brief experience, and nothing more than a matter of business? For Greg, anyway. But oh, yes — to answer her own question, she definitely wanted to see him again.

He was opening the door of the taxi for her. On impulse, she leaned towards him and brushed his cheek with her lips.

'I'll help you. I will find out. Trust me.'

He grinned. 'Good luck.' He closed the door after she climbed in.

The taxi driver said, 'Where to?'

'Oh — yes.' She gave him the address, turning to where Greg was raising his hand, still smiling. He hadn't seemed fazed by her gesture, had he? But not particularly encouraging either.

You fool, she told herself, *he probably thought it was nothing more than his — sealing the deal.*

But he had kissed her. Properly. How did he feel about her? Really?

No, he was more concerned about the task before her and whether she would be able to prove his innocence. Of course he was.

Familiar streets. They were almost there. Here was the street where her flat was. The flat she shared with Stephen.

Oh, no! It was far too soon. Stupidly, she had wasted valuable time wondering about Greg's feelings and her own instead of working out how she was going to tackle this. What was she going to say to Stephen?

Cat hardly heard the driver's question.

'Yes, just here, please.' She paid him and thanked him without thinking. Taking a deep calming breath as she climbed out, she looked up at their window. A figure was looking down at her — Stephen presumably. She smiled and raised a hand. The figure moved quickly away.

Of course, he would be running down to open the front door, wanting to throw his arms round her. That would take him less than a minute.

Cat fixed a smile on her face — and waited. There was no sound of his footsteps on the stairs. No sound of anything. What was he thinking? Since she hadn't had her bag with her keys since the ill-fated hen night, she could hardly let herself in. Although, be fair, perhaps Stephen didn't know that. She rang the bell.

Even so, it seemed an age before anything happened. Her smile faded. What was he doing?

And at last, the door opened.

'Cat! That's great.' Before, yes, flinging his arms round her.

She mumbled, 'I'm so sorry,' into his T-shirt. 'I don't know what happened. I haven't got my key. It was in my bag.'

'That's OK. Your bag's here. In the flat.' He turned and began walking up the stairs, hanging onto her hand as if he couldn't bear to let her go in case she disappeared again. And who could blame him?

He said, 'I've been so worried. I didn't know what to think.'

Cat took a deep breath.

'We need to talk,' she told his back.

'Yes, of course. Come in. Sit down.'

She tried another smile. 'Thanks. I do live here.' She waved the bag she'd bought in the charity shop. 'I'll just dump this in the bedroom and take my medication. Luckily I've had no ill effects from three days without it.'

Coward, she told herself. *You're just putting it off. You have to get on with it.*

Stephen frowned. 'Why? What's in the bag?' He was blocking her way with one arm.

Cat laughed awkwardly. 'I had to get some new clothes. Hadn't you noticed? I couldn't go round in that pink number all the time. Not very practical.' Now she was quoting Greg, more or less. She wished he was here to help her out. Or just wished he was here, full stop.

Had there been a noise in the bedroom?

'What was that?'

Stephen laughed too, his laughter sounding no more natural than hers had.

'What? Nothing. Just dump that on the sofa and come and talk to me in the kitchen. I'll make coffee. Are you OK?'

She followed him. No doubt she was imagining things. She was feeling too edgy.

'Yes, thanks. I am now.'

'We've been very worried,' he said again. 'We didn't know what to think.' He pushed the kitchen door closed behind her and began filling the kettle. And now Cat could hear someone coming up the communal stairs to their door.

Nothing surreptitious about these steps.

He said, 'Ah, that will be Amanda.'

'Oh, good.' Cat couldn't wait to see Amanda. Now she would discover Amanda's version of what had happened. However, her arrival at this exact moment wasn't too convenient. This would put a stop to everything Cat had intended to say, just as she had been gathering the courage.

She stepped back, out of the kitchen, before the kettle had even come to the boil.

Amanda too was all smiles, opening her arms.

'Oh, thank goodness. What a relief! I said you'd get back, though, didn't I, Stephen?'

Something didn't seem quite right.

88

Yes, that was it. Amanda didn't have a key, and yet they hadn't heard the bell. How had she got in?

And there was something a bit odd about the way she'd put that. Cat said carefully, 'What do you mean? Get back from where?'

Amanda dropped her arms and stepped back.

'Oh, Cat, I'm so sorry. I shouldn't have said anything, I know, but when Stephen was so upset at your disappearance — I just had to tell him.'

'Tell him what?'

'That I'd seen you leaving with someone. A tall, dark, thin man with a beard.'

'What?' Cat stared at her. Whoever could that have been?

'I thought you must be having a last fling. It often happens, doesn't it? No one blames you.'

'But I didn't. I wouldn't — ' She stopped abruptly. Wouldn't she? What about her feelings for Greg? Was that so very different, even though nothing had happened? Apart from those kisses. Her face was growing hot.

Amanda said gently, 'Come and sit down. I'm sorry if I've upset you, but seriously — how much about your hen night do you remember?'

'You must know better than I do. Hardly anything. Somebody spiked my soft drink, I'm certain of it. After that I don't remember a thing.'

Stephen sat down on the sofa, next to her, on the other side. Cat felt trapped and hemmed in.

'The thing is, Amanda and I have been talking about this.' His voice was quivering. 'If you've changed your mind about marrying me, please say.' He paused. 'After all, when we were coming up the stairs, you said we needed to talk. Was this what it was about?'

Cat put her hands to the sides of her head, as if that would help her to think.

'Yes, we do. I meant it. But I don't know any tall, thin men with beards. Not that I can think of. And you're right, I don't remember what happened but I'm sure I didn't sleep with anyone.'

Amanda said quickly — too quickly? — 'No one blames you if you did. It's quite understandable.'

Cat said slowly, 'I need to tell you what I do remember of what happened.' She paused. Even though Amanda was here and this wasn't quite how she'd pictured this conversation, surely now was the time to tell them everything she and Greg had agreed she would say?

She was no longer certain, however, that this would be a good idea. Something about Stephen's response when he opened the door hadn't rung true. Someone had seen her from the window as she got out of the taxi. She had heard someone in the bedroom; Stephen had stopped her putting her bag in there. And how had Amanda got in without ringing the bell? Either Stephen had given her a key — or she had been in the flat already.

Cat decided to be careful what she said. She took a deep breath.

'It's all very odd. When I came round, I was on a small island off the coast of North Wales. And there was a bad-tempered guy there who seemed to know who you were, Stephen. In fact he seemed to know who I was, too. And he thought you must have sent me there, with a message of some sort for him. I didn't know what he was talking about.' She paused, thinking. 'He was tall and dark, but broad-shouldered rather than thin. And he didn't have a beard.'

Stephen was shaking his head, looking puzzled.

'He said he knew me?'

Amanda said sharply, 'And then what? How did you get back? And it's been three days. Three days, Cat.'

Was Amanda hurrying her past the inconvenient parts of the story? Cat was determined that she wasn't going to be hurried — or distracted.

'You know the effects alcohol can have on me with my medication. Or the theory of it, since I'd never put those instructions to the test. Not until now. Just as well, it seems, because I felt very ill when I first woke up. I was totally out of it for those days that are missing.' She stopped again. 'And getting back wasn't that simple. I got back as soon as I could.'

'How?' Amanda demanded.

'Like I said, it wasn't easy. First I had to convince that person who said he knew you that I could be trusted.' She wasn't going to tell Stephen Greg's name that easily. She wanted to see what he was going to admit to. 'Only then would he help me to come back. And of course, I had no bag, no phone — nothing like that.' She was watching them carefully but they weren't exchanging suspicious glances or anything like that. They were giving her no clues at all. OK then — she wasn't going to give them everything either.

She said, 'Anyway, how does it matter how I got back? I'm here, aren't I?' Still no response. 'But if it's so important, he helped me get back to the mainland, borrowed a vehicle and then I got a taxi.'

It looked as if Amanda was going to

leap in again and no doubt with another distracting and irrelevant question. Amanda could wait. Cat wanted to hear from Stephen. She said quickly, 'What's all this about, Stephen? I think you know more than you're saying.' She stared straight into the pale grey eyes, waiting.

Amanda stood up abruptly and went to the window. Stephen shuffled his feet, unable to meet Cat's gaze. Yes, Cat thought, that had been the right way to play it.

Stephen coughed.

'What did you say his name was?'

'I didn't. I was assuming you'd know.' She stared directly at him. 'No? Have you forgotten?' She was counting on Stephen's all-too-expressive face giving him away. And yes — he was looking away, refusing to meet her eyes.

She continued, 'His name was Greg.' Stephen looked up, startled. 'Were you expecting someone else? No, of course you weren't. And it's obvious that you recognise the name.' But his surprise did seem genuine. Perhaps she was being unduly tough on him.

Yes, she had changed her mind and knew now that this intended marriage had been a huge mistake — but that was hardly Stephen's fault. And whatever had gone wrong, there had been a fondness, even a kind of love between them. It wasn't easy just to dismiss that without feeling anything at all.

Cat said, more gently, 'He said you would know who he was.' Something, perhaps an unwitting flicker of Stephen's eyes, made her turn to look at Amanda, who had been pacing the room and was now standing directly behind Cat.

As Cat turned, she caught Amanda nodding at Stephen, eyebrows raised. But she smoothly included Cat, changing her expression into a smile of encouragement.

Very cleverly done, Cat thought. *But why is Amanda being like this?* It wasn't like her at all. Or were the events of the last few days making Cat paranoid, so that she was imagining things?

Stephen said, 'Yes, I'm afraid I do.' He moved closer to her, holding her hand gently, stroking her fingers in a caring way. 'I didn't want to tell you. I wanted to protect you from all this. It wasn't long before we first got together, after — well, never mind all that.'

Cat thought, *When Amanda finished with you.*

He was hurrying on, 'We first met when you were on the short term work exchange with your office in Germany. Remember?'

'Of course.'

'Everything was happening so fast when we first found each other. And you were taken up with your work in Europe, and we didn't get much chance to talk about my work, what I was doing.'

'No, we didn't.' But that hadn't seemed like an omission. She had been swept away by the moment and trying to help him. No time to ask much about what he did for a living. Not in any detail. And he'd probably assumed she would know already, with Amanda being her best friend.

But Amanda had never really said much about Stephen when she and Stephen had been an item. Apart from telling Cat how gorgeous she thought he was, and being vague about everything else.

Cat said, 'It didn't seem to matter. I knew it was something to do with IT, of course.'

'We didn't need to publicise our business much,' Stephen said. 'We seemed to be achieving maximum impact through social media and word of mouth.' He hesitated. 'And then, when it — the disaster — happened, it hit me hard. It was just so devastating. I didn't want to talk about it and you never mentioned it. You couldn't have heard anything about it. Amanda didn't seem to have told you. And I thought it would be best to keep it that way. Besides, with losing Amanda as well, so soon after — I just couldn't cope with it all.'

'When what happened?' Cat asked.

'This Greg — he didn't mention it?'

Cat didn't want to release too much of what she knew too soon. And obviously from the way Stephen was fencing around with his questioning and vague answers, neither did he.

She said, 'I need to hear this from you, Stephen. He didn't mention what exactly?'

Stephen hunched his shoulders. Perhaps he was giving in. 'I should have told you, I suppose. But you didn't want to talk about your work much; you said it was boring admin mostly — and it wasn't hard to let you think mine was the same.'

Cat shook her head. 'It sounds as if I should have asked more questions.'

'I suppose I should have told you. But Cat, falling for you was so joyous, after everything I'd been through — ' Behind them, Amanda coughed. He said quickly, 'I wanted to concentrate on grabbing happiness where I could. But yes, there were three of us running

98

our business — Greg, Vincent and me.' He frowned. 'Surely I told you that much?'

'I can't remember. I don't think you did.'

'Anyhow, I was getting worried about how things were going. Vincent handled all the financial aspects. I was admin, like I told you. But something didn't seem right, though I couldn't quite pin it down. Ask Vincent a question and the answer sounded reasonable — and when you thought it through later, he hadn't answered the question at all. I think Greg was concerned too, though he hadn't really said as much. So I went round to Vincent's flat one night, hoping to sort things out once and for all.' He swallowed, turning away from her with a hand over his eyes. 'The door was standing open and I knew that wasn't right. I went in — and Vincent was dead. He was lying on the floor. And Greg was there too. He'd killed him.'

'What?' Even though Cat had known

this was coming, hearing it from Stephen was disturbing. He seemed to have leaped to conclusions very quickly.

Stephen was shaking his head. 'I know. It was a terrible shock.'

'How did you know Greg had done it? I mean, couldn't it have been an accident? Or a burglary gone wrong?'

'No. He had Vincent's blood on his hands. Literally. And when he saw me, he shoved me out of the way and ran.'

Cat stared at him. 'Ran?' she repeated, her face blank. She wanted to say, 'Are you sure?' She stopped herself. She mustn't give too much away too soon. But this was nothing like Greg's account. She said, 'What about the police? What did they say? You see, I didn't think — I mean, Greg didn't seem that sort of person.'

'Who does? Who knows what anyone might do when provoked? Presumably he'd got Vincent to admit to something he didn't like and just lost it.'

This was no help at all. And somehow she must get Stephen to tell her something useful. She was on difficult ground here.

'But what about the police?

'The police?' Stephen's face was expressionless.

'Surely you called them? You must have done.'

Stephen shrugged. 'Like you said, a burglary gone wrong was all they came up with. Obviously they never got anyone for it. Bungled things, if you ask me — but just as well for Greg.'

'So was anything taken?'

'Ah. Apart from Vincent's laptop? Not in the way you're meaning. The thing was — I only realised after Vincent was killed that the business account had been cleared out. I didn't know what to think. Had Vincent moved it on and concealed it? I don't know. I've never been able to track it down.'

'Money? But — ' Cat was shaking her head now. She had to pretend she'd never heard about the money but she was no good at this. 'Has it never turned up?'

'No. And now that you've found Greg, I think I need to ask him some questions.'

6

'Questions,' Cat repeated. *Pull yourself together*, she told herself. 'I don't understand.'

'Yes.' Stephen sounded to be gaining confidence. 'Where has all that money gone? There's no sign of it. It seems to me Greg may know something about that. Presumably that's why he went round to see Vincent. And he must have been the last person to see him alive — so what did Vincent tell him?'

Cat shook her head. 'You're leaping to conclusions without any real evidence. And Greg didn't say anything about money to me.'

Stephen gestured wildly. 'He wouldn't, would he? But if he doesn't have it, who does? No wonder he's gone to ground, hiding from me, knowing I have an equal claim on it.'

'Do keep calm,' Cat said. 'I'll tell you

what he told me, if you'll just listen. Greg said he recognised me when he saw me, said he'd seen my photo on your phone, with Amanda. That you showed him who I was when you and Amanda first got together. He was pleased to see me, genuinely so — I'm certain of that. He thought I'd come with a message from you. He'd been waiting to hear from you. As you'd promised him.'

'He actually said that?'

'Yes, I told you.' If this was a pretence, he was being very convincing. He looked as confused and surprised as she was feeling. 'And of course,' Cat continued, 'I didn't have a message from you or anyone. I didn't know anything.' She thought, *I wish I had done. I could have been far more helpful*. 'I don't know what to make of all this. Are you absolutely sure you can't tell me anything?'

'No.' He was shrugging and looking everywhere but at her. Not so convincing now.

'Besides,' Cat said suddenly, 'how did I get there? I'm not buying this bearded stranger story. Can you look me in the face, Stephen, and tell me my sudden appearance on Greg's island was nothing to do with you?'

He slid his face towards hers.

'Yes, I can. Of course it was nothing to do with me. How could it be?'

'You tell me. It seems a very strange coincidence if not.'

Amanda said sharply, 'Can you not remember, Cat? Anything at all about how you got there?'

Cat jumped. With Amanda standing so quietly behind her, Cat had all but forgotten she was there. Perhaps it was just as well that she was. Perhaps she could help to make sense of all this.

'No. You know, don't you, how my consultant always told me I could be adversely affected if I had any amount of alcohol? Well, he was right. In fact, it was worse than he'd always suggested. I've no idea what happened. I can't even remember much of that evening before I had anything to drink. It's just a fog.'

Amanda wiped a finger beneath her eyes. There was a catch in her voice.

'I'm so sorry, Cat. I don't know how that happened. I didn't know you'd been anywhere near alcohol. And I was supposed to be looking after you! Can you ever forgive me?' She flung her arms around Cat again. 'I was desperately worried about you when you didn't come back the next morning. It's so good to see you again, safe and well.'

Cat returned the hug although it seemed to be going on for a little too long. And she had a strange feeling of being two people at the same time — the old Cat who had been Amanda's best friend for so long, and a new, suspicious Cat who could do nothing but seek out flaws in everything anyone said. It was happening again, now. Because what about the noise in the bedroom and Amanda getting in here so quietly?

She moved back. 'Yes, safe and well.

And without that fog in my head so I can think straight again. There are things I need to do. Did you tell the police I was missing? Because I'll have to notify them that I'm back.' She managed a smile. 'I don't want them sending out search parties, do I?' *And Greg would want that even less.*

Now there was no disguising the cautious way Stephen and Amanda were looking at each other. Or Amanda's slight nod before she spoke.

'No, we didn't tell them. Which turns out to be just as well, doesn't it?' She laughed. 'We might all have been accused of wasting police time.'

Cat didn't share her laughter. Amanda became defensive.

'No, like I said, I thought you'd gone off for a last one-night stand fling and that you'd be back. No one any the wiser.'

'And you let me go? Didn't you realise what kind of state I was in?'

'The thing is, you didn't seem any different. I hadn't seen you drinking and you were walking OK and talking normally. I just thought you'd be back. I'm sorry, I know this comes as a shock. But I have to tell you what I saw.'

Cat stared at her. She knew suddenly that Amanda was lying. 'What you saw? Was it you who saw this man — or did someone else tell you about him? And if so, who told you?'

She felt a huge sense of betrayal. Why was Amanda lying? Anger swept through her.

'Or maybe this whole thing has been quite convenient? For you two.' The words rushed out before she could think about them. Or stop them.

Supposing she was wrong? She wouldn't want to hurt Amanda. But if she was right, then Amanda hadn't been too worried about hurting her.

Oh, no, this was dreadful. Amanda was her best friend. She was about to say, *No, I'm sorry, I didn't mean that*, when the look on Amanda's face stopped her. For a fleeting moment, mixed in with Amanda's horror and concern, Cat was certain she had identified a look of guilt. She had known Amanda for too long. Though not quite as well as she might have thought, it would seem.

The look was gone as quickly as it had appeared. Had she imagined it? Amanda shook her head, now looking only sorrowful.

'I don't know what you mean. I really don't, I'm afraid. Are you sure you're not still confused? Understandable after all you've been through.'

Cat straightened her back.

'No. I'm not confused at all. Not now. I'm seeing things quite clearly.' She looked directly at Amanda, willing her to admit that she and Stephen were back together. Because that must be why she was already here.

And that would solve all Cat's problems. She was foolish to feel aggrieved and betrayed; better to have everything out in the open because it would be the answer to everything and with the minimum of distress. If she

109

waited long enough, perhaps one of them would come out with it.

The two were still looking at her, saying nothing. The silence was becoming painful.

No, she told herself firmly. *I'm not going to chicken out of this. It has to be done.* She took a deep breath.

'I'm sorry, Stephen, but I have something to tell you. I must have been thinking about this for a while — at some deep level. Not admitting it to myself. And then when I was completely out of everything, I realised — it came to me when I woke up.' She swallowed. 'I knew then that I can't marry you. I've made a terrible mistake.' She looked down at her knotted fingers and looked up again, to catch Stephen and Amanda exchanging glances. Cat ploughed on, 'I know this will come as a shock. Or I thought it would. I'm so sorry.'

Stephen said, 'I don't get it. What do you mean?'

Amanda cut across him. 'Don't say

anything you're going to regret, Cat. Please think about this. You're probably still affected by the meds and the drink.'

Stephen was nodding. 'It's all been too much. Meeting up with Greg in that strange way — and then there's the man you seem to have left with. Who was he? No wonder you're confused.'

Cat put her hands to her head.

'No, no. It's nothing to do with all that. It was never right, you and me, that's the point. You were on the rebound, Stephen. I should have known that was wrong from the start — and with Amanda being my best friend too. I should have had the sense to keep right out of it until you were both sure of your feelings.' She shook her head. 'But you were in such a state, Stephen, and I couldn't bear to see anyone suffering like that. I wanted to help. I thought I could at least listen to you and be sympathetic and ease the situation as far as I could. And somehow it all got out of hand.' She didn't feel she could look at Amanda. 'I thought I was falling in love with you. You told me I was and that you loved me too.' How pathetic and feeble she sounded. As if she didn't have a mind of her own. 'And it all happened so fast.'

Amanda's voice was cool. 'Are you saying this supposed love affair was all Stephen's fault?'

'No, of course not.' Cat paused. That was what she was saying. But he had been the vulnerable one who was in no state to think things through sensibly. She should have had the sense to stand back, particularly when she began to see what was happening. 'But at least I've realised in time. Before we took the final step. That would have been very wrong.'

Stephen was wearing his hard-done-by look.

'This has all been a terrible shock for me. I hope you realise that. After everything I've been through. I've nothing left.' He wandered moodily over to the window and then turned suddenly. 'And this is your flat! I moved in with you. You won't want me here any more, will you? That's quite clear. I'll have to move out.'

'I don't know. I'm sorry. I hadn't thought of that. Yes, I suppose that would be best.'

'Where am I supposed to go, then?'

All of a sudden Cat lost her temper.

'You can move in with Amanda. Since that's obviously what you both want.'

'Just be quiet, Stephen,' Amanda snapped. 'Let me and Cat talk to each other. Alone.' Without giving him time to argue, she gestured Cat into the kitchen and shut the door.

Not much room, Cat thought. The kitchen was tiny — but the bedroom would hardly have been a tactful choice, would it? After all, how long had Amanda been staying here? Perhaps there were tell-tale possessions of hers strewn around in there. Cat didn't try to hide her anger. Why should she?

Amanda, however, enveloped her at once in another tearful hug.

'Oh, Cat, whatever must you be thinking? I'm so sorry. But it wasn't like that. Stephen and I aren't back together. We wouldn't. Of course not. He was so upset when you disappeared; you know what he's like. I was trying to console him.'

'I see,' Cat said grudgingly. And she did. Since Amanda was only repeating the excuse Cat had made only a few minutes ago, Cat felt she could hardly argue.

'I just had to help him through it. I was doing my utmost to persuade him everything would be all right and you would come back.' Amanda paused, standing back a little, still with her hands clasping Cat's shoulders. And yes, those had to be genuine tears in her eyes. Didn't they? Cat wanted to believe her.

Amanda was saying, 'And he was coping so well. But now you've changed your mind after all. I don't know how he'll react.'

Cat felt as if she was on a see-saw. A few minutes ago it had seemed as if Stephen was willing to accept her decision — and now suddenly she was to blame for everything.

'Amanda, I just don't know what's going on. I have no idea how on earth I found myself on a small, out-of-the-way island in North Wales. But I am quite certain that none of it was my fault.'

Amanda leaned closer, her voice low and urgent.

'Listen, we have something more important to worry about. However it happened, you've met this man, Greg, who used to be one of Stephen's partners. I expect you know that.'

'I do now. I didn't know before. I'm sure Stephen never mentioned any of this.'

Amanda was almost whispering now. Surely she was being over-dramatic? Even if Stephen had his ear pressed to the other side of the door, he wouldn't be able to hear.

'Did Greg tell you he was on the run?

Accused of murdering their other partner?'

'Yes.' Cat wanted to tell her Greg was innocent — but no, she must wait and see what Amanda was going to say.

'The thing is — no one's ever discovered what happened to the money in the business account. And it's important that we find it.' Amanda nodded, solemnly.

'Yes, of course — but isn't it more urgent to discover who killed this other person? Vincent, was it?'

'Oh, Cat, isn't it obvious? If we find out who has the money, we will have solved the murder.'

'I suppose so,' Cat agreed doubtfully. You'd think Amanda was talking about solving some kind of puzzle. But someone had died. And although Cat had never met him, she assumed Amanda must have known him. She said, 'It must have been very upsetting. Did you know him well?'

'What? Oh, I'd known him as long as I'd known Stephen, naturally. But he

116

was more of an acquaintance than anything else. I can't say I ever liked him much. I tended to avoid him. But what I thought about him isn't really relevant, is it? We need to find the money and sort all this out. You and I together. Just as we've always been.' She laughed, raising her hand in a high-five.

Cat responded reluctantly. 'Yes.' Part of her ached to be back onside with Amanda. She wanted to be swept away by what Amanda was suggesting. Perhaps they could work together to solve this horrible series of events.

Amanda was saying, 'Because Stephen and Greg haven't made much of a showing between them, have they? They're getting nowhere.' She lowered her voice again. 'And maybe there's a reason for that.'

'A reason?' Cat shivered. 'You don't mean you think it was Stephen?'

If so, why was Amanda getting so close to him? Surely that was a dangerous thing to do.

'Maybe,' Amanda muttered. 'Or

Greg, obviously. Don't forget him.'

Forgetting Greg was the last thing Cat was about to do. She didn't know what to think now. When she had been with Greg, everything had seemed so straightforward. She had believed every word of what he was telling her. Was that because she *wanted* to believe him? Swept away, maybe mistakenly, because she was so attracted to him? That was ridiculous. Cat had only known him for a few days. She had to be sensible.

Amanda glanced at the door again.

'I think that if you split up with Stephen, as you're suggesting, we've lost our chance to find the money.'

'And the truth,' Cat said.

'Yes, yes.' Amanda waved an arm as if dismissing the truth as a dispensable extra. 'Stephen needs to stay here with you and then you can question him and find out exactly what happened.'

'Yes, I see what you mean — but I don't think I want to be . . . *together* with him. Not now.'

'Oh, I'm sure he isn't dangerous.

Even if he did it, he wouldn't hurt you. Oh, I see — you mean you don't want to be physically close to him any more? Having discussed your decision. Not a problem, he can borrow my airbed and sleep in the sitting room.'

Cat tried to think of an argument against this. It wasn't what she wanted to do at all. Amanda was smiling encouragingly.

Cat said, 'Wait a minute. If he moves in with you, *you* can ask him the questions. And I get the impression that's what you both want. Because you've been staying here anyway, haven't you?'

Amanda ignored the inconvenient question.

'Not possible just now, I'm afraid. There's someone else staying in my flat at the minute. There isn't room. You know how tiny it is.'

'Who?' Cat demanded. She must not allow Amanda to push her into this. No way.

'Just some of the overflow wedding

guests,' Amanda said airily. 'Some of them had made the effort to travel quite a distance, if you remember. They'd always planned to stay a few days more and explore the area.'

Cat gave up on that. There was no point in arguing about it. And Amanda *had* offered accommodation, she seemed to remember. Whether these guests existed or not, that wasn't the most important thing right now.

'We have to discover the truth,' she declared. 'That's what matters.'

'Yes, we do. And having been so close to Stephen since then, you're the best person to do it. We need to find out whether Stephen killed Vincent. You must see that.'

Cat was shocked. How could Amanda have been renewing her relationship with Stephen if she really thought he was a murderer?

'Surely you don't think that when you've been so close to him?' She didn't add, *and still are.*

Amanda was rushing on. 'It has to be

somebody. You must see that. Stephen can't be ruled out. We have to approach this methodically. Although obviously, it would be wonderful if we could rule him out.'

Cat shook her head.

'I don't think this is a good idea.'

'Look, he's feeling very vulnerable just now, after everything that's happened — and if you let him stay here after all, he'll be so grateful that it will be easy to get him talking. About anything and everything to do with it, so we can get to the bottom of it all. '

'Has he never spoken to you about what happened? You were still close to him at the time, weren't you?'

Amanda pulled a face. 'I've asked him since, more than once, but he just shrugs me off.'

Cat knew she was clutching at straws.

'It will be very awkward, having him still living here after I've made my decision.'

'All the better. Awkwardness will engender openness. If you can just get him going — arguing even — who knows what he'll come out with?'

'I don't like it. It seems very manipulative.'

Amanda laughed. 'Oh, Cat. This is what I've always loved about you. You're so sweet and forgiving. If Stephen is guilty of anything, manipulating him is justified.' Somehow she was managing to make 'sweet and forgiving' sound like undesirable qualities.

Am I? Cat thought. *Obviously not much help when trying to solve a crime.* And who were these guests who were preventing Amanda allowing Stephen to move in?

'Did I invite these guests who are staying with you?' she asked suddenly. 'Who are they?'

'Guests? Oh, no. Friends of Stephen's. No one you know. I'll tell you what, they know everything's at sixes and sevens now. I can easily move them on in a day or two and if you're making no headway with Stephen, he can come over to me then.'

Cat sighed, unconvinced. She was almost certain Amanda had invented all this to get her own way. When Amanda was set on something, she would always come up with some convoluted method of achieving it. So often with a smile and a hug, so that Cat would find herself crumbling. She was doing that now. Cat smiled and hugged back, unable to help herself.

Oh, well, there was no point in arguing about it and perhaps it made some kind of sense. Cat was supposed to be gathering information for Greg — and how could she do that if she wasn't seeing much of Stephen? Far better to listen to Stephen's account herself instead of relying on someone else, even if that person was Amanda. It could end up like a game of Chinese whispers and Amanda's version of the facts could be influenced by her own interpretation.

Cat sighed again. 'OK then.'

'That's great.' Amanda was beaming. 'This will be the best way, you'll see.'

She flung the kitchen door open. 'Stephen, you're staying here for now. Just until I can get everything sorted out. Cat's going to borrow my airbed for you and you can have it here in the sitting room.'

'No need, I've got the sofa bed,' Cat said.

'So that's agreed then. Brilliant. See you soon.' Amanda gave Stephen a quick hug too, without the slightest hint of self-consciousness. 'Bye.' She was gone.

Cat and Stephen were left staring at each other. Where was she going to start?

'OK,' Stephen said. 'There are a couple of things we need to talk about.'

Cat flushed. 'I know. I'm sorry.'

Oh dear, she didn't want to wade through all the inevitable recriminations about the wedding and her change of heart. She had let him down badly and when he was already distressed and vulnerable. At the worst possible time. But of course she would have to.

She said, 'I'll make my sofa bed up for you.'

If these mystery guests did exist, they would need Amanda's airbed, wouldn't they? Amanda hadn't thought that through.

Stephen brushed a hand through his hair.

'Good grief, there's plenty of time for that. That's not what I meant. No — it's something else.' He paused. 'You said you've met Greg? So where is he now?'

7

Cat stared at him. 'What? I thought you knew where he was. I mean, he isn't there now anyway. I don't know where he is.'

She was telling the truth but felt her face redden, only too aware that the phone Greg had given her was burning a hole in her pocket.

Stephen regarded her thoughtfully.

'Of course you don't. I believe you. He'd be stupid to tell you where he was going, wouldn't he, knowing you might tell me? And assuming he believed you — if you told him about everything being over between you and me and the wedding being off. You did, didn't you?'

'Yes,' Cat admitted, knowing that telling Greg before telling Stephen didn't seem to have been the best thing to do. 'It was because he was there. And I suddenly knew. I had to tell someone.'

126

Stephen shook his head. 'That doesn't matter much now. As I was saying, Greg would be very unlikely to do a stupid thing like that, because he certainly isn't stupid. No way. Not when he has all our money stashed away somewhere — and killed Vincent to get it.'

Cat opened her mouth to leap to Greg's defence, managing just in time to change, 'No, he didn't,' into 'What makes you think Greg killed him?'

She was out of her depth. This wasn't the Stephen she had thought she knew and had fallen for, the vulnerable person she had wanted to protect and care for. This was a strong and organised version.

Stephen was saying, 'I told you. I found him with Vincent's body and he ran. Leaving me to cover for him.'

She tried to choose her words carefully.

'And didn't he say anything?'

'Not that I remember.'

'But I thought you knew where he was going. I thought you had organised everything.'

Stephen gave a short, hard laugh.

'Looks like you've been told an interesting version of events. No, I didn't. Obviously it was better that I didn't know — just like you, now. What I didn't know couldn't be divulged.'

Cat didn't feel convinced. He didn't seem to be telling her much at all. He must have been able to remember more than this. She tried to work out how to express it in order to get the most from him — but he was already saying, 'So where was he hiding, then?'

No harm in telling him that. Greg wouldn't go back — there was nowhere habitable to go back to. 'I woke up in a cottage on a little island — off Anglesey, I think it was. There were two together, used by conservation wardens. Greg was living in the other cottage. When he found me — '

'What about that man you left with? The night before — or however long it was?' He was looking at her with narrowed eyes.

She continued steadily, knowing she

128

was on safe ground now. 'I know nothing at all about him. If he existed at all — because I'm beginning to wonder. As I was saying, when Greg found me I was still out of it. The effects of someone spiking my drink, probably with alcohol. You know I mustn't drink. I told you as soon as I met you. I don't know how it happened that I did. I felt ill for quite some time after I came round. I wasn't well enough to leave straight away . . . ' She hesitated.

'Yes?' There was a dangerous note in Stephen's voice.

Cat was thinking fast. Surely it would do no harm to tell him about their three pursuers? He knew about Vincent's family already. She would leave it to Stephen to make the connection.

'It seems there were other people after Greg too. They set fire to the cottages. Fortunately, we were able to get out.' She shuddered. So far she had hardly had time for the horror of that ordeal to sink in. 'We got away before they saw us.'

'That seems convenient.'

'Well, they came after us and caught me — but I escaped.' Should she have told him any of that?

He was giving her that suspicious and searching look again. 'Who were they?'

Cat felt a wave of anger sweeping over her. He hadn't bothered to ask if she had been OK. Or whether they had hurt her. She snapped, 'They didn't say.' If he couldn't work that out for himself, she didn't see why she should help him.

Stephen jumped up to look out of the window at the street below. 'Do they know you're here?'

'No. Or I don't see how they could know.'

Stephen muttered, 'I don't like this.'

And you think I do?

The phone in Cat's pocket vibrated. Stephen was still looking out of the window. Cat turned away and read the text quickly.

Meet me outside in 10. She slid it back.

130

Too late. Stephen was watching her. 'Who was that?'

'One of my friends. They've all been frantic.'

'You don't have to tell me. Your phone's in your bag, on the table. There. It's been going non-stop — until it ran out of charge.' He paused. 'I didn't know you had another.'

'I had to get one. Since I didn't have mine.'

'But you didn't think to ring me on this new phone? I was frantic with worry too. Amanda and I both were.'

'I know. I'm so sorry. But that was all part of this decision I've made. I had to think things through.' She added belatedly, 'Besides, I didn't have your number.'

'I can recite yours.'

'I know. But I don't have that kind of brain. You know that.'

'Hmm.' He shrugged, a sceptical look on his face. 'And I don't suppose there was much time for thinking — not with the three musketeers chasing after you.'

It was obvious he didn't believe her. She said sharply, 'You're right; it got complicated. But everything I've told you has been true. Whether you believe me or not makes no difference. And now I am here, I agree, there are dozens of people I need to contact so I'd better get on with it.'

She had an idea. She knew what she was going to do. 'But first things first, if that's all right with you. I'm starving. What have we got in the fridge?' She strode into the kitchen. 'As I thought,' she called, over one shoulder, 'almost empty.'

Stephen was wrong-footed now and looking bemused, as well he might.

'Hang on — we were worried sick. We had no idea where you were. Mostly we got take-outs delivered. I didn't even want to leave the flat to eat, in case you turned up. Shopping was the last thing on my mind.'

'So I can see.' Cat flung the fridge door closed and began dramatically opening and shutting cupboards.

'We were going to be away, remember? On our honeymoon. This isn't like you, Cat. You're being unreasonable. It's as if a different person has come back.'

'I think I am a different person. It's because I'm seeing things more clearly. Anyway, I'm hungry and I need to go to the supermarket.'

Stephen said, 'Right, then. I'll come with you.'

Cat's eyes widened. *Oh, no. That won't do.*

'That's very kind. But there's no need.' She leaped on to the attack again. 'You're saying *I'm* different? What's all this concern about? You don't usually bother about the shopping.'

'Usually? This isn't usual, is it? You might not come back again.'

'Of course I will.' Cat hoped that was true. 'I have to, don't I? What would I do with all the food, otherwise?'

'It might not be up to you. What about those three villains?'

Cat stared at him. 'Oh, you suddenly believe in them, do you? I told you — we lost them.'

'You don't know that. You can't be certain.' Stephen was looking out of the window again. 'How did they find you in the first place?'

Cat went to stand beside him. There was no one there. Of course there wasn't.

'You're making me jumpy now,' she said crossly. 'And they never wanted me. They were after Greg — ' She bit her lip. This was going in the wrong direction. Stephen was distracting her. She didn't want him to be thinking about Greg.

Stephen said, surprisingly, 'OK, you go, then. You're right. I'll stay here to sort the folding bed.'

Cat wasn't going to question that. She shot over to the door before he could change his mind.

'Bags?' he suggested, raising his eyebrows.

'Oh, yes. Nearly forgot.' She snatched

134

the shopping bags from the kitchen drawer. Because she would have to do some shopping, wouldn't she? She would just have to be extra quick.

'Handbag?' He was grinning now.

'Yes, that too.' She took her bag from the table. 'I won't be long.'

It was only as she reached the street that the doubts really kicked in. Why had Stephen changed tack so easily? She glanced up at the window. Yes, he was still there, watching her. She waved up at him, trying to appear casual before walking away. Forcing herself to walk very slowly. No — that was even worse than jogging would be. *Walk normally*.

One thing she had always liked about her flat was the proximity of the small supermarket. Five minutes from the nearest corner — which was here at last and now, as she turned that corner, Stephen could no longer see her.

She looked round. No sign of Greg yet. Where was he? It was safe to approach her now. She'd better get the promised shopping. What had been left in the fridge? She couldn't remember. It hardly mattered, did it? Just concentrate on the basics. Bread, milk, eggs, fruit, salad.

She looked round again. Where was Greg expecting to meet her? It must be more than ten minutes now. Better send him a quick text as she walked. Because here was the supermarket, and he wouldn't know where she'd gone.

Cat had hardly pressed Send when Greg appeared beside her, walking in step. She couldn't prevent a warm smile. But no, she had to concentrate.

'Oh! Hi. You startled me then.' *Don't give him a chance to speak*. She carried on, rapidly, 'I can't be long. I've said I'm shopping. I'll get some bread and milk and eggs and stuff while you talk to me.' She took a wire basket as they entered the shop.

Greg's voice was grim. 'Change of plan. I don't want you going back there.'

Cat glanced up at him, frowning.

136

'But that's where I live.'

'And what about Stephen?'

'He's still there, for now. But he's not staying long. We had it out between us — and with Amanda too, because I'm certain they want to get back together. Which lets me off the hook. As soon as Amanda has room, he'll be going back to hers.'

'No. Not good enough. You can't be there with him.'

Cat shrugged. 'You're right, I didn't like the idea of it at first. Not when I've changed my mind. But then I realised how this is for the best. It's giving me a chance to find out more. We've hardly touched on what happened with Vincent so far.'

'But you have mentioned it? What did he say?'

Cat sighed. 'He said it was you who killed Vincent. He said he was certain of it.'

'And do you believe him?'

She paused. 'I don't think you did it, if that's what you mean. But Stephen may genuinely *believe* you did. Some of what he said, and the way he reacted, did ring true. I can't give up now. I need more time.'

Greg groaned. 'It's too dangerous. I don't know what I was thinking of, putting you into this situation. I should never have suggested it.'

Cat tried to sound matter-of fact.

'No, it's understandable. After all the drama and excitement of what we'd just been through together, it was the best thing we could come up with. And even though things have calmed down now, I still think so.'

'You have to come with me. Now. Please, Cat.' He took her arm and she almost dropped a box of eggs.

'Greg, that's ridiculous. What will Stephen think if I disappear again? He and Amanda would be on to the police straight away, in a panic. We were lucky they didn't do that last time.'

'Somehow, I doubt that.'

She said firmly, 'No. We need to prove your innocence and I'm not

138

leaving until I've got more. Even if he genuinely thinks you're guilty, Stephen might be able to tell us more about Vincent. Anything he'd been doing that may have led to what happened. Anything he may have said to give us a clue. Anything that can help us.' She glared at Greg and he glared back.

He put his hands on her shoulders, looking at her as if trying to remember her face. 'If you came to any harm, I would never forgive myself.'

Was he going to kiss her again? No, he mustn't do that. She stepped back. She wanted that to happen, but it would only complicate things even more. Blood was pounding in her ears.

'I have your phone.' She swallowed. *Keep calm*. 'If things start to look bad in any way, I'll ring you at once. I promise.' She added, 'But I still can't believe Stephen would do anything to hurt me. And I don't think he would be capable of murder anyway.' But what about her uneasy feelings that Stephen was different now?

139

Greg made a huffing noise, resignation or irritation maybe. 'Yeah. That's what I thought you'd say. I've known Stephen for a long time and he didn't seem much like a murderer to me either. And like you say, he can probably give us more insight into what really did happen, even if he hasn't realised that himself.' He straightened his back, as if making a decision. 'All right, then. But ring me if you need me — any time, day or night. At the slightest sign of any trouble. I won't be far away. In fact — no, better leave it at that.' He turned and was gone.

Cat frowned after him. What had he been going to say? If she hadn't had this basket of stuff to check out, she could have gone after him. But no, she would have only been drawing attention to them both. The last thing she wanted.

She packed the shopping into the familiar bag she always used, and began the familiar walk back to the flat. Everything seemed so *ordinary*. As if none of the events of the last week

140

could ever have happened.

Perhaps they hadn't. Perhaps she'd imagined it all, or dreamed it. Perhaps she was still in a fantasy world brought on by the medication.

Cat was even muttering to herself as she climbed the stairs. *Greg is being ridiculous. How can he even suggest I could be in any danger from Stephen?* She was glad Greg had all but admitted that himself — eventually. It was quite possible that Vincent's death had been an accident. She really needed to get some sensible information on that. No more messing about. She would begin straight away.

She opened the front door and called out.

'I'm back, Stephen.'

There was no answer. Where was he?

She shook herself. He'd be somewhere about and she had to put these things away. Perhaps he'd suddenly thought of something else they might need and dashed out. Stephen was like that. He would have hoped to catch up with her and missed her in the aisles. In which case, she hoped he hadn't noticed Greg.

Anyway, she thought as she quickly dumped everything out of the bag and pushed the milk into the fridge, *never mind where he's gone. This is a heaven-sent opportunity to do some research.*

She opened her laptop. Of course, it must need charging — and where was the charger?

No, the battery was showing full. That was odd. But no doubt Stephen had been borrowing it. His was getting unreliable now, and high time he updated it — or so he was always telling her.

What she needed was a factual account of what had happened, as reported at the time. She tried to work out some promising keywords. Not easy. She didn't even know Greg's surname. And where had the three of them been living when they were running their business?

Ah, but she knew the victim's name, didn't she? That brother of his had obligingly told her. Bryston. Vincent Bryston. An unusual name. She knew roughly the time of year when it had happened — when she had been working in Germany. It should be really easy to find.

She stared at the screen.

8

The intercom for the outer door bleeped. Cat was still staring at the screen as she picked up the handset. 'Yes?'

'Parcel delivery for Stephen Wright.'

'Thanks.' What had Stephen been ordering? She released the door and went back to the search engine.

Oh, come on. Where could the news item be? Perhaps if it was down as an accidental death, the national papers wouldn't have been interested. But even if the nationals hadn't picked up on it, surely the local papers should have covered it? If there had been any kind of search for Greg, that should have made the headlines.

Nothing. Not even to say he was wanted for questioning.

Well, hadn't Stephen told Greg he would sort everything? That could have meant anything. And having met the Brystons, she could imagine that maybe they weren't too keen on involving the police anyway. But in that case, why was Greg keeping a low profile on that island? It didn't make sense. Unless he was avoiding the Brystons rather than the police.

The door opened. Without turning, she said, 'Just put it down anywhere, please.'

No answer — and now she did turn.

'Greg! What are you doing? You can't come here. Stephen will be back any minute.'

Greg came in, closing the door behind him.

'No, he won't.'

Cat felt her face freeze. 'What do you mean?' Ridiculous thoughts flashed through her head. 'Did he see you? Was he waiting for you? Did you have a fight?'

Greg didn't look as if he'd had a fight. He looked just the same. Whatever had happened? A sinking feeling was appearing below her ribs.

'No. He didn't see me. But those three who were following us saw him.'

Cat gasped. 'They were there?'

'Yes. I came out of the supermarket and something made me hang back and wait in the doorway of the newsagents next door. I saw you come out — and then Stephen. He'd obviously been following you. I don't know if he'd seen us together in the supermarket. But if he had, you'd think he'd be following me, not you. So I followed him, to see what he was going to do next.'

'I didn't know,' Cat murmured. 'I should have thought of it. I should have turned round.'

'Just as well you didn't. He didn't, either; he had no idea I was behind him. I kept at a safe distance. And then a white van pulled up next to him and two of those jokers shot out — even at that distance, I recognised them — and bundled him into the back.'

Cat's eyes were so wide that they felt painful. She blinked, relieving the dry ache, and swallowed.

'When they took me, they were asking which of you two had the money. They must have decided Stephen has it.'

Greg's face was non-committal.

'Or perhaps it was just luck. That they happened to catch sight of him first.'

'Oh. I see.' She gulped. 'What do you think they'll do to him?'

'You know better than I do.'

'But surely they're unlikely to hurt him — or not much? If they do anything too bad, they'll never find out what they need to know, will they?' The words *if they killed him* seemed to be hanging in the air between them.

'Let's hope they see the sense in that.'

Cat shivered. Sense wasn't a word she would have associated with the two who seemed to be subordinate to Dean Bryston. How much control did he have over them? She was remembering the chill in their voices as they had discussed whether to throw her over the cliff or not.

'I don't think — Greg, we can't just leave him with them, can we?'

'It's not ideal, no.'

Her mind was racing. What could they do to help him? Calling the police was the last thing Greg would agree to. Unless . . .

She said, 'I know you wouldn't want to have anything to do with the police but perhaps I could call them? Without involving you. Because I don't think the police are bothered about me.' She stopped. 'Oh, of course — you won't have realised. It seems nobody reported me missing.'

'Really? Why does that not surprise me?'

Cat paused. 'I don't know what you mean.'

'And there again, it does surprise me. Leaving Stephen and Amanda out of it because who knows what on earth is behind their actions for much of the time, what about the other guests? And your parents? Haven't they missed you?'

Cat bit her lip. 'There's only my dad. He tends to be — a bit judgmental. He

148

decided straight away that he didn't like Stephen. And it got worse when we were marrying in such a rush, as he saw it. We had a big row and we haven't spoken since.' She paused again. 'Stephen was very reassuring. He said we didn't need my dad to be there if that was how he felt. And there was so much to arrange. I meant to try and make it up with him after the honeymoon — when he'd cooled down a bit and saw what a good husband Stephen could be.' She sighed. 'Ironic, considering how it's turned out. Seems like my father was right all along.'

'He should be pleased, then. When you tell him.' Greg's voice was dry. 'And your friends?'

'Well, Amanda found my bag with my phone and I expect she must have dealt with any queries.'

'From everything you've said about her, that wouldn't surprise me either.'

'It was the only thing she could do, wasn't it?'

'How long have you known her?'

Cat frowned at him, surprised. Why was he being so critical of Amanda?

'Why? I've known her for years. We were at school together. Even before that.'

'Do you trust her?'

'Of course! You can't be thinking — ' No, it was unthinkable. She hurried on, 'This thing she's had with Stephen, getting back with him — I mean — perhaps I should have kept away from him altogether even though she'd dumped him. I just felt so sorry for him. He was so distraught. He wanted to talk about her all the time, with someone who knew her well. Naturally.'

'Naturally,' Greg echoed.

'That's how it started. At that time, I hadn't seen them together in a normal situation. I hadn't been around when she met up with him. I was already away. Perhaps I would have been more wary if I had, and never got mixed up in any of this. I was in contact with Amanda, of course, and she told me all about him when we were phoning or

150

Skyping. I couldn't wait to meet him, I was so happy for her.' She shook her head. 'I so wanted to meet him and things kept cropping up to prevent him coming over. Something always seemed to come up with the business.'

'Yeah, that did happen a lot,' Greg said. 'For all three of us. With it being a new venture, we poured all our time and energies into it, 24/7.' He laughed, without amusement. 'As it turned out, some more than others.'

Cat took a deep breath. She had to say it.

'You mean, because of what happened to the money?'

He gave her a sideways glance. There was a brief, awkward silence. Was he trying to work out what to say? Was he suspicious of her now, wondering why she was asking?

She wanted to blink and look away but she fought against it. She made herself keep looking at him with her eyes wide open.

'Yes.' His voice was giving nothing

away. 'I presume you know it's gone?'

'Yes.'

'And how exactly do you know that?'

Cat took a breath. 'Those three villains told me. When they seized me. They want it back.'

'Back?' Greg raised his brows. 'It was never theirs in the first place. They might have a case to claim Vincent's third — assuming all of it was come by honestly, anyhow, which I doubt.' He paused, frowning. 'Hang on, this must mean Vincent didn't have it. That's odd.'

'Or they didn't *know* he had it. He may not have included them in what was going on.'

'You're right. I wouldn't be surprised about that. Vincent didn't have much to do with his family when we were at uni. Never seemed to mention them much. Though he threw a party at their house once, when it was empty. When he did let slip a few facts about them, later on, I wasn't surprised he hadn't said anything earlier.' He was silent, thinking. 'But surely Vincent must have had the money? I'd assumed that was why he was killed. Or part of the reason.'

Cat shook her head, trying to clear her thoughts. It didn't help.

'They made it very clear that they think either you or Stephen has this money.' She shivered. 'And will stop at nothing to get it.'

He looked at her sharply. 'They scared you, didn't they? Did they threaten you? I should have asked you about all that earlier.'

'Well — they did threaten me, yes, but I don't think the older one who seemed to be in charge would have let them push me over the cliff or anything like that. They were just trying to frighten me, as you said. Dean, the older one, who was dressed like a businessman, thought they could use me as a bargaining tool and negotiate with you and Stephen.' She smiled. 'But you distracted them very cleverly, with the explosion, and so it never came to that.'

Greg was frowning. 'Just as well, since I don't know where the money is.

How should I? I wasn't in control of that aspect of the business. I was research and marketing.

'Although there's no way the Bryston family will understand this, the money isn't my major priority. Finding the truth and clearing my name are what matter most to me. If we recover the money along with that process, fair enough. Except that some of it would come under the definition of criminal gains, I suspect — ' He shrugged. 'It doesn't matter. I really don't care about it now.'

Did Cat believe him? She wanted to, but she wasn't sure. He sounded convincing — but she didn't know who to believe any more.

She said tentatively, 'You seem very casual about it. You must have worked hard, after all, helping to build the business. Making a contribution. You don't strike me as the sort of person who would stand back when anything needed doing.'

Greg paused. 'No, you're right. I wasn't. I threw myself into it. I was committed, enthusiastic.' He gave her a wry smile. 'But what was it all for? I'm not even convinced the venture as a whole was entirely above board, and that was never my intention. I was so busy concentrating on what I had to do that I ignored the bigger picture. And apart from all that — the thing is, Cat, that this whole experience has changed my life and the way I see things. The way I think about life altogether.'

'Yes.' She nodded thoughtfully. 'I can see that. A shocking experience like that — discovering Vincent's body and your friend being convinced you'd killed him — would affect anyone.'

'It's not just that. I needed a bolt hole, somewhere to hide while the heat died down — as I thought.' He grunted. 'And when another friend I got hold of told me about the island and how there was a vacancy for a live-in warden there, it seemed ideal. And it was. It was great. I thought I'd miss the bustle of business life, online meetings, organising the deals — but I didn't miss it at all. Not any of it. It was a completely new experience for me. For those few months, I was living a very simple life. Just the basics.'

'Were you the warden of the island in general?'

'No. I was tasked with caring for a rare orchid that grows there. I just had to check that the plants were OK several times a day and divert any unwelcome visitors. There were ropes round the sensitive areas, which were all away from the paths. It was an easy job. And you know what? I liked it. I liked being on my own with the sea and the sky, watching the sun rise and set, listening to the calls of the seabirds.'

'Didn't you feel lonely?'

'Maybe I was beginning to wonder why Stephen was taking so long to get back to me — but as the weeks passed, I found that I didn't care too much. I might have changed my mind when the winter came.'

'Would the orchids need protecting in the winter?'

'Good point. Probably not. But none of that matters now, does it? Because everything kicked off and everyone arrived at once. First you, and then the other three.' He added, 'And that changed everything.'

Cat couldn't read his expression. Did he mean in a good way? No, he couldn't mean that — not after everything he'd said about the idyllic life he'd been leading there.

She said, 'I'm sorry. I suppose it did. And for me as well.'

'The cottages are presumably no longer habitable after that fire. I don't know if the conservation group in charge will be able to fund their repair.' He seemed to be immersed in the practical aspects of the situation. 'Maybe I could use a tent . . .'

'But you can't go back at all, with the Brystons after you,' Cat repeated. 'And going to the island has made everything different for me, too.'

'Yes. I see that.' He brushed her shoulder lightly with one hand. 'You had a lucky escape, by the sound of it. Whoever brought you there did you a good turn.'

Cat knew she had to say something.

'Do you regret it? I mean, me being dumped on you like that? I didn't intend that anyone else should be dragged into all of this.'

He smiled. 'Unless it was a coincidence, it looks as if somebody intended exactly that. We'll just have to see where we end up, won't we?'

Was there tenderness in his eyes? Did he mean he didn't regret meeting her? Cat wished she knew. She had thought at first that he, too, had felt a spark of something between them. Particularly when he had kissed her.

She nodded. 'Yes, we will.' But there were other things they should be worrying about now.

Greg was crossing the room to look out of the window, concealing himself behind the curtains. He was looking down at the street.

Cat thought, *Yes. What have we*

been doing, wasting time like this? She said suddenly, 'We can't stay here, can we? It isn't safe.'

'I don't see how they would know your address. I'm presuming Stephen had moved in with you?'

Cat sighed. Yet another rushed decision.

'Yes, he had. It was all just so over-whelming. And exciting. I didn't have time to think.'

'I'm not questioning your motives. I'm just thinking that since I didn't know your address, I don't see how the Brystons would know it.'

'Oh.' Her spirits sank again. 'But Stephen didn't live far away, when he was with Amanda. No more than a couple of streets. The Brystons only need to keep an eye on the general area.'

Greg was staring out of the window again.

'Clever move on Stephen's part — if he had something to hide. Covering his tracks so they couldn't find him that easily?'

Cat wanted to leap to Stephen's

defence but the words stuck in her mouth. Had Stephen ever loved her at all — or had he just been making use of her? Her heart sank at the unwelcome thought. No, there was no point in worrying about that now. They had to concentrate on their current situation.

'If they have Stephen, they can make him tell them this address.'

Greg raised his eyebrows. 'I would hope he'd have more consideration for your safety than that. Surely he would attempt to protect you?'

'That might depend — ' Cat paused and swallowed. 'It could depend on what they were doing to him. Or what they threatened him with.'

Greg gave her a searching look.

'It was worse, when they had you, than you were letting on, wasn't it?'

'No — not really. I mean, it could have been if you hadn't come to the rescue.'

'And you think Stephen would give way under similar treatment?'

Cat shook her head. 'I don't know.

160

I'm not sure of a lot of things right now.' She straightened her shoulders. 'Except that I don't think we should hang around to find out. I'll get a few more things packed, quickly. And what about you? Where are you staying?'

He grinned. 'I've just taken a very small room in the building next door. Right at the top.'

She nodded. Of course. The one with the scruffy *Rooms To Let* sign and the live-in landlord who never seemed to go anywhere.

'Good idea. A bit of a waste as it's turned out.'

He shrugged. 'You never know. Could be useful later. And it's very similar to this building and has a back door — so I would think this one will have one, too?'

'Yes. Ah, I see what you mean. A better way to exit.' She went into the bedroom again. Somehow she had become amazingly calm. She packed a few basics, including toiletries and a fleece. *Comfort and warmth*, she thought. *Prioritise.*

161

She was out again in minutes, feeling pleased with herself, although Greg was already looking at his watch. He frowned as she darted into the kitchen. 'What are you doing?'

She was stuffing her backpack into a clean black bin bag. He understood at once.

'Good idea. Anyone watching will think we're taking rubbish out. I'll get one too.'

Cat locked the front door to the flat behind them as they came out onto the landing. She shivered. Would she ever come back here? Would she ever see her little flat again? She had loved living here. *Stupid*, she told herself. *Get on with it*.

She led the way down the stairs and out of the back door at the end of the rear ground floor corridor. She looked up and down the narrow alley behind the houses. 'It's OK.'

Greg opened the identical door leading to the next house. 'I made sure the bolt was undone before I came round. But we'll bolt it behind us.' He

162

unlocked the peeling back door and ushered her in. It didn't close easily.

Cat didn't think the splintered wood could have withstood a determined attack. Well, they would just have to hope it wouldn't have to withstand one. And why should it? They weren't going to be here long either. *Think positive.*

Greg ushered her inside and she followed him up the creaking stairs, avoiding the broken handrail. Past the level her flat was on, next door, and up into the attics. Her building had an attractive self-contained flat up here, but this had two separate rooms off a bare landing with an unsavoury-looking bathroom. The whole house smelled of damp.

She wrinkled her nose. 'I'd heard it's going to be refurbished soon. It changed hands quite recently. He could do with getting on with it.'

'Lucky for me he hasn't started yet. I've only got it on a temporary basis — and the paperwork was non-existent.' Greg unlocked one of the doors and they hurried in, as he locked it behind

163

them and strode over to one of the roof light windows. Cat stood next to him.

'It's a good view. Lucky you overlook the street.'

The road was empty. Cat found herself relaxing a little. Surely they would be safe here? How could anyone know where they had gone? And the Brystons and Stephen would assume they would have gone as fast and far as possible.

'We could stay here.' She was thinking aloud.

'We would be trapped.'

'Oh, I see. But if one of us watched the street continuously? We'd have plenty of time to get out of the back door if we saw them.' She frowned, doubting herself. 'Wouldn't we?'

'Too easy for them to see us. They could have somebody guarding the alleyway, watching your building. An elementary mistake if they didn't.'

And Dean Bryston didn't make mistakes. Cat sighed. 'I suppose so. You're right.'

He said, 'Right, I'll pack. Not that

I've unpacked much here yet.'

She took his place at the window. Nothing. She thought, *It would be so good if we could only stop running and pause for breath.* She glanced up at Greg. Would she rather be relaxing on her own, with her life as it used to be — or on the run with Greg? *Don't be silly, she told herself, you're falling for him and you've only known him five minutes.*

Still nothing. There wasn't even much traffic. No — here was somebody! She gasped. It couldn't be. Stopping at her outer door, letting himself in. There could be no mistake.

'Greg! It's Stephen. He's going in, next door.'

'What?'

Greg didn't seem very surprised. Cat almost wished she hadn't said anything. She was trying to consider his reaction. Because after what Greg had witnessed — or had told her he'd witnessed — how had Stephen got away from them so quickly?

Had Greg really seen Stephen being bundled into a white van by the Brystons? But why would he lie about it?

'Stephen,' she repeated, stupidly, pointing down to the now empty step.

Greg frowned. 'That doesn't seem right.'

'No. That's what I was thinking.' Cat's phone rang. She jumped, snatching it from her pocket, glanced at the display. 'It's him!'

'You'd better answer it, then.' Greg seemed far calmer than she was. He smiled. 'Maybe don't tell him where you are?'

Cat nodded. 'You're right.' She took a deep breath before answering. Stephen was almost shouting. It was easy for Greg to hear him too.

'Where are you?'

'Why? Where are you?'

'You're not in the flat.'

'No.' Cat thought quickly. 'When I got back, you weren't there. I was worried. I've been looking for you.' She raised her eyebrows at Greg. 'Wait

166

there, Stephen. I won't be long. See you soon.' She cut the call before he had a chance to argue. 'So we'll go now, shall we? There's nothing to wait for. We can be quite a distance away before he realises I'm not going to turn up — ' She stopped. 'No. This is ridiculous. What are we doing?'

Greg was nodding as if following her thoughts.

'You're right. I've had enough of this. Keep running and we'll get nowhere. And I'm not running from Stephen. It's time we faced him.'

Cat's hands were clenched in determination.

'You're right. I agree. But what about those other three? And what you saw?'

Greg smiled grimly.

'I don't think we need to mention them. Not at first. Let's see what Stephen has to say.'

9

Cat nodded. 'Yes, let's — though it isn't quite what I meant. I'll be interested to hear his version of what happened. I want to know where those three are now and what they're doing.'

'Oh, yes.' Greg nodded. 'That's essential. Because however he's got away from them, whether he's given them the slip or whatever — ' He paused. 'They'll know your address now.'

'I don't like the sound of that.' She shivered without intending to. 'Or the *whatever* option.'

'Neither do I. But let's hear what he has to say and face that when we get to it.'

Cat suggested, 'We need to meet him in a public place. Very public.'

'Agreed.'

Cat lifted the phone again. 'Stephen?

I'll see you at the Central Square. By the fountains. There's something I need to do first.'

'What?' Stephen objected. 'Why there?'

'Just do it. I'll explain later. See you in ten.' She ended the call.

'Good choice,' Greg said. 'So let's go.' He grinned. 'And we'd better make sure he doesn't see us.'

That was not difficult. Stephen had no idea of concealing himself as he left the flat next door and strode along the pavement, talking into his phone. They followed their original plan of leaving by the back door, although that hardly seemed necessary. As they hurried along the alleyway and rejoined the main road, he was still ahead of them, unaware of their movements.

'Who's he phoning now?' Cat muttered. 'It's taking a long time.'

'Exactly. Who indeed? Could be innocent chit-chat but I don't think we'll take that chance. And we'll hope it isn't the Brystons.'

If Stephen was trying to fulfil some

169

sinister plan, he wasn't going about it too cleverly, Cat thought. Unless he knew they were behind him and was leading them into a trap.

Was Stephen capable of doing something like that? Cat didn't know. She didn't feel she knew what anyone was capable of any more — or who she could trust.

Greg was continually glancing over his shoulder, as she was, looking for the Brystons' white van. There was no sign of it. And now the ten minutes was up and they had arrived.

Stephen came to a halt, by the fountains as instructed, gazing around the square.

Cat's phone rang. Stephen sounded mildly irritated. 'Where are you? I can't see you. I'm in the square now.'

Greg mouthed at her, making a negative swishing gesture with one hand. Cat nodded. She said, 'Sorry, change of plan. Stay there and I'll let you know. In a few minutes.' She cut him off.

They watched him frowning as he slid his phone back into his pocket.

Cat murmured, 'He doesn't look to be telling anyone about the change. If that was what he was doing last time.'

'You can't be too careful.'

Not where the Bryston brothers were concerned. Cat bit her lips together. But what if Greg had invented the whole thing? She only had his word for it about Stephen's abduction, if that was what had happened. Had she been gullible to have believed it? It did seem unlikely. But why would he invent something like that? She didn't know. Everything was happening too fast and they didn't seem to be getting any-where.

'OK,' Greg muttered. 'I'll come up behind him while you cut across by the shops and confront him.'

Cat nodded. 'Right.' She didn't ask Greg what he was going to do. One glance at the determined expression on his face was giving her the idea that it would be something Stephen might not welcome. Obviously, however, being in such a public place would provide protection for Stephen as well as for them. Or so she hoped.

She broke into a jog. Stephen wasn't looking towards Greg but to make sure of it, she waved and called out his name.

He turned to face her.

'Oh — there you are. What's going on?'

Cat took a deep breath.

'Exactly. That's what we need to talk about.'

'I don't get it. Why bring me out here — and following a random trail of instructions?'

'Not quite a trail. The thing is — ' Cat paused as if catching her breath.

'Don't you trust me?'

Cat breathed a sigh of relief as now Greg had appeared behind him, putting a hand on Stephen's shoulder.

He said, 'No, I don't think we do.'

Stephen was trying to twist away but Cat was directly in front of him; she noticed how Stephen winced as Greg's grip tightened and his other hand grasped Stephen's arm. Cat had a perfect view of the expressions chasing across Stephen's face. He was worried and fearful but trying to hide it. Cat knew him too well to misread him.

He muttered, 'You! Greg! I didn't expect to see you here. What do you want?'

Greg smiled. No one would have guessed, amongst the busy crowds shopping and sightseeing, that anything was wrong. He said, pleasantly, 'Some answers, I think.'

'You want answers?' Stephen blustered. 'What about me? You killed Vincent.'

'We both know I didn't. If anyone killed him, it was more likely to be you.'

Stephen had turned a little, giving all his attention to Greg. Or so they were supposed to think, Cat realised. But she could see how he was trying to slide one hand round to his back pocket. She reached over and gently removed his phone, out of reach of those clutching fingers.

Greg said, 'When I last saw you, Stephen, you said you would help me. Although I admit it isn't easy to remember after I'd had that blow to the head. But you said you would see what you could find out about what had happened to Vincent. That was several weeks ago and you've told me nothing.'

Stephen said quickly, 'I did help you. I didn't call the police.'

'Why not? It might have been helpful to me if you had. It couldn't have been much worse.'

'I never gave up on you. And we'd always been good mates, the three of us. I didn't think you could have killed him deliberately, whatever you thought he'd done. I decided it must have been an accident.' He paused. 'So I cleaned everything up as best I could — and then left.'

Cat was shocked.

'What — you just left him there?'

'I knew it wouldn't be long before

someone found him,' Stephen said quickly. 'His brothers, maybe.'

'Ah, yes. His notorious family. What did they make of it, I wonder?'

'I don't know, do I? I didn't see them.'

'You tell me. Didn't you?'

Cat said again, 'You just left him there? You could have called them, couldn't you?'

Stephen was silent, looking from one to the other as if trying to weigh up what they would believe. 'Well, yes, I did. I called them anonymously from a phone box. You remember, Greg, there was one near Vincent's flat. So no, I didn't just leave him. Nothing like that.'

'Odd that you seemed to have forgotten about that. And you don't know how they reacted because you didn't hang around to see?'

'Yes, you've got it. How could I know what they did? I haven't seen them since. They can be a bit in-your-face when they want to be.' Stephen tried to laugh. 'I knew they wouldn't be happy about the way he'd died. Not at all. No, mate, I've kept well out of their way.'

Greg placed an arm around Stephen's shoulders, in what could be interpreted to a casual passer-by as a friendly gesture. 'Well, as it happens, Stephen, *mate*, I've been keeping an eye on you myself. And I saw the Bryston brothers — helping you, shall we say? — into their van. It would've been — ' He glanced at his watch without removing his arm from Stephen's shoulders. 'About an hour ago now. So what did they want?'

* * *

Amanda was sitting in her empty flat, thinking. There was a lot to think about. Was everything still going to plan? She had an annoying feeling that events were slipping out of her grasp. She had to regain control, and quickly.

Which of course was what she thought she'd been doing in getting back with the devastated Stephen. She thumped a fist on her knee. Only three days in

176

which she had been 'consoling' him — what a wimp he was — and yet he had been no help at all.

No surprise that he had made no sensible effort to search for Cat, and just seemed to think he must wait until she turned up. Far more importantly, Amanda was almost convinced now that he knew nothing. Or nothing that mattered. He couldn't even manage to have the conversation with Cat without seeking help. He had left three messages on her phone now, which Amanda was deliberately ignoring. Let him cope on his own for a change.

Because she had tried everything she could think of. During the last three days, she had been gentle and supportive, stroking his forehead.

'Stephen, love, please tell me the truth about what really happened that night. I'm sure it all comes back to that.'

But he'd just sat there moaning and shaking his head. 'Where is she, Amanda? Where has she gone? I can't live without her.'

Amanda had also tried being angry and threatening again, which of course was why she had dumped him in the first place. Hoping to jolt him out of this ridiculous and unnecessary secrecy. But he just hadn't got it.

She sighed. Maybe she was wrong. Maybe he didn't know anything. Or maybe he was much cleverer than she'd ever thought, and the stakes were far too high to allow him to let things slip.

Perhaps he had killed Vincent. He didn't seem capable — but maybe this continual weeping and wailing was all an act.

Cat, perhaps, thought so. She seemed not to fancy being left alone again with a possible murderer. Amanda gave a sharp, humourless laugh. Cat might have already been in exactly that situation, since Greg was certainly the other suspect. She didn't seem to have worried too much about being alone with him!

But then, as usual, Cat would have

been in her own little bubble of unreality, never having realised there had ever been a murder or that Greg or Stephen had been in any way involved.

Amanda stood up quickly, her movements fuelled by irritation. If she had known where Cat would end up, would she have acted as she had? But knowing nothing at all about it had seemed the best option. And now Cat, who should just have been removed from the whole thing, was more entangled than ever.

What if Cat and Greg became an item and he knew where the money was? Amanda gave a frustrated howl. Even worse — and understandable. There was none of that little-boy-please-help-me stuff with Greg, all that self-pity which made Stephen so irritating. Amanda knew she could never have had a long term relationship with Stephen, even with the money easing the way.

But — but — could Stephen ever have been ruthless enough to commit murder? Her thoughts had brought her back to where she'd started. Not good enough. Oh, perhaps she had better see what he had been sending her messages about. She snatched at her phone. And then she would take action and sort it all out.

* * *

Stephen glanced around uselessly as if seeking some kind of inspiration.

Greg said, 'Yes?'

Stephen's expression changed. Cat turned. Behind them a small red car was careering across the square, with tyres screeching as it dodged the pedestrians. Cat shouted a warning as it jerked to a stop next to them. The door shot open.

Amanda. Cat felt weak with relief. Amanda was leaning forwards from behind the wheel. 'Get in, quickly. All of you. They're coming.'

And yes, just as Greg had described, a white van was entering the square from the far side.

Stephen leaped into the passenger seat. There was no time to think. Cat climbed into the back and slid over. 'Greg?'

He spared the time to look at the van before following and slamming the door.

'This will be Amanda, then?'

'Yes.' Although that hardly seemed to matter.

'Get down,' Amanda cried.

They obeyed. 'Your best friend, as described?' Greg murmured. Cat's head was squashed against his knees.

'Yes.'

Greg raised his head a little. 'Good to meet you, Amanda. Where would we be without friends?'

They were swerving away through the square although all the pedestrians seemed to have scattered, understandably. Now they were out onto one of the exiting streets. Cat hung on grimly. There would be more point in telling Amanda to drive more carefully, she thought, than introducing himself — but Greg seemed remarkably calm.

Amanda had found a gap in the city traffic and their headlong flight was slowed, with an irate hooting of car horns. Greg sat up, glancing back.

'That was an ordinary delivery van, Amanda. They're unloading carpets, by the look of it. I'm surprised you didn't realise it wasn't a danger to us, Stephen. Because you got a good look at the Brystons' van.' He paused. His voice was pleasant, conversational. 'But you knew all of that, didn't you, Amanda?'

Amanda turned to glare at him.

'If you're so clever, why did you get in?'

'To see what would happen if we did.'

'So now you've found out,' Amanda said. 'And yes, I have a plan. And I thought you might argue about it and we haven't time to be arguing. OK, that was just an ordinary delivery van but the Brystons are out there somewhere nearby and the longer you three spend wandering around in full view like that, the more chance there will be of them spotting you. A huge chance, wouldn't you say, Stephen?'

Stephen hesitated. Cat could almost have felt sorry for him. No, she decided, she didn't.

'You came to an agreement with them, didn't you, Stephen? You were going to betray us to them?' she snapped.

Stephen found his voice at last with the words coming out in a rush.

'It wasn't like that. They thought it was, but I was going to be stringing them along.'

'A dangerous game,' Greg observed.

Cat said, 'But thanks to Amanda, we have avoided all that. And it sounds as if you have a plan too, Stephen? Can we have more details?'

'Plan? I wouldn't call it a plan. I had to think fast. They were very aggressive. I knew I had to convince them that I was on their side. That I wasn't the enemy.'

Cat nodded. And why not? Hadn't

she tried to do the same thing?

Greg said, 'And they believed you? All too easy, wouldn't you think?'

Stephen nodded quickly. 'Yes, I know. You're probably right. I shouldn't think they trust me at all. But I didn't care. They let me go. That was all that mattered.'

'And now they'll be following you,' Greg said, 'which will lead them to us. And as Amanda has helpfully pointed out, they won't be far off.'

'It's OK,' Amanda said. 'I can lose them. Wherever they are and whether they're watching us now or not. Hang on.' She tossed her hair back as she leaned forward over the wheel, a determined look on her face.

Cat was gripping the door handle as instructed. She thought, *I don't like this. All this running and hiding. I just want it to stop*. And yet Amanda seemed almost exhilarated as she twisted and turned. Yes — she was actually enjoying this.

They were all silent as the car

184

traversed the city streets, manoeuvred through the suburbs, found a slip road and joined a dual carriageway, finding a gap that was hardly there, without slowing.

Cat spoke at last.

'Amanda, where are we going?'

Amanda laughed. 'We've lost them. I'm certain of it. I told you I could.'

Cat snapped, 'You know exactly what you're doing, don't you? This wasn't just a random choice of directions to put the Brystons off our track. If anyone has a plan, it's you.'

Amanda laughed again.

'You know me too well.'

Greg's voice was abrupt.

'I'm sure Cat does. Or thinks she does. So let's hear it, shall we? Since this plan, whatever it is, obviously affects us.'

Amanda swung the wheel, overtaking at speed.

'I get the feeling you don't like me much, Greg. And I can easily guess what that's all about.'

'Let's hear it, then.'

Greg's grim tone didn't disconcert her at all.

'It's about how everything went wrong on the hen night. But that wasn't really my fault. And let's face it, it all turned out for the best, didn't it? Otherwise, Cat might never have realised she'd made a mistake. She and Stephen would have been married now. How catastrophic would that have been?'

'Thanks,' Stephen muttered.

'Come on, Stephen, it would have been a mistake for you too.' Amanda slid a hand across to his knee. 'I know that better than anyone.'

'Amanda.' Greg's voice was filled with menace. '*Where are we going?*'

10

Cat could see Amanda glancing in the driving mirror; gauging Greg's expression, maybe?

'OK, you'll know soon enough anyway. It's a holiday cottage belonging to my family. Or was. Not far from Harby Point.'

'I thought a lot of that land belonged to the National Trust?'

'Not this bit. Perhaps it got overlooked. The coastline is always shifting with the sand — and the cottage has literally been buried in sand more than once. My uncle gave up on the idea of renting it out eventually. No one ever goes there.'

'Sounds ideal.' Greg's voice was sarcastic. 'Yet another isolated cottage as a destination. That worked well last time.'

'Obviously I can take you anywhere

you want — but being in the middle of a city didn't work either, did it? Trust me, no one will ever find us here. And it's not long term. We just need somewhere to put our heads together and regroup.'

Cat said, 'I think we have to, Greg. For now, anyway. All this running is getting us nowhere.'

'I certainly agree with that part of it. Right then, Amanda, if we can choose an alternative — I've just seen a sign to Woodmere. That would be my choice.'

Stephen's head jerked round. 'What?'

Cat felt she was the only one who didn't get it.

'Why? What do you mean?'

Greg squeezed her hand. Reassuringly? Meaning, *don't worry, I know what I'm doing*?

Amanda said carefully, 'There's no point. They will still be driving around ten miles away, looking for us. Waiting for Stephen to contact them. None of them will be there.'

'All the same. I'd like to try it.'

'Look, we're almost at the cottage now.' Amanda was at her most persuasive and reasonable. 'Like I said, let's go there, pause for breath and discuss all the options.'

Cat's phone vibrated. She took it out, frowning as the number Greg was using appeared on the screen. Greg nudged her arm, sharply, and she dropped the phone.

'Sorry, Cat,' he said.

Cat dived down to retrieve it, hampered by her seat belt, and almost bumped heads with Greg as he did the same. He breathed into her ear, 'Trust me.' She read the text he had sent her. *Pretend to faint.*

'Got it?' Greg was saying, sitting back. 'Sorry about that, Cat. Anyone important?'

Cat shot up, so quickly that she hardly needed to pretend. 'Just PPI — ' She gave a stifled moan, hoping she sounded convincing, and flopped against Greg.

He was saying, 'Cat? Cat, are you

OK?' He put an arm around her, supporting her. 'What's the matter?'

'It's all been too much,' Stephen said angrily. 'She needs looking after, not all this chasing about. She'll still be suffering the after-effects of everything she's been through. And she had no medication for three days.' Surprisingly, he seemed to be directing his anger at Amanda.

Just as well, Cat thought, as Amanda would be hard to convince without Stephen's back-up.

Greg was fanning her face, tapping her hands. 'Cat? Do you want a drink of water? She needs water, Amanda. We'll have to stop and get some.'

'There's some in the back. In the pocket behind my seat.'

'Where? Oh, this. No, it's almost empty. And how old is it?'

'Oh, all right.' Amanda sounded reluctant. 'I could do with some petrol anyway.'

Cat closed her eyes again, moaning a little as they pulled into a petrol station. Amanda's voice was suddenly nearby;

she must be peering at Cat's face as she leaned through the gap in the front seats.

'I don't like the look of her,' Greg muttered. 'She feels very hot.'

Risky, Cat thought. Supposing Amanda tested the truth of that? Fortunately she didn't. Instead she was saying, 'Splash that bit of old water on her face and I'll get some more in a minute.'

Stephen's voice now.

'No, she doesn't look good at all.' There seemed to be genuine concern in his voice. Cat felt sorry for him. But no doubt he would find out soon enough that she was all right, when Greg's plan was revealed.

'Right,' Amanda announced briskly. 'You get the water, Stephen, while I fill the car. That will be quicker.'

Stephen was still hesitating. Through her eyelashes, Cat could see that he was glancing across at Amanda. 'And I want — ' Whatever it was he wanted, he must have thought better of it as he flung open his door and set off at a run.

191

He still hadn't emerged, however, before Amanda had finished at the pump and was setting off to pay.

'What's he doing?' Cat muttered, half opening her eyes. 'Is there a queue?'

'Seizing the opportunity to talk to Amanda on her own, I expect. Right, yes, she's in the shop too — and guess what, she's left the keys here.'

'What?'

With a swift, agile movement, Greg was out of the back seat and into the front, behind the wheel.

'Greg!' Cat jerked herself upright. 'What are you doing?'

They were speeding away, joining the traffic as quickly as Amanda had.

'That's excellent! We've done it.'

'You've just stolen Amanda's car.'

'Just borrowed it, that's all. Don't tell me you preferred her plan? Because I certainly didn't.'

'Well, no. But what if they call the police?'

Greg laughed. 'I don't think that's likely. The police don't seem to feature too strongly in any plan of Amanda's.'

'But what will they do? They're stuck there.'

'I wouldn't feel sorry for them if I was you. They'll think of something. Or Amanda will. Hard to say whether Stephen will contribute much to that — though you never know. I'm beginning to wonder whether Stephen has hidden depths.'

Cat sighed. 'You're talking in riddles.' And perhaps, not for the first time, she felt that she was out of her depth and perhaps she could have done with that water after all.

'Maybe so — but then, all of this is one big riddle. Full of unexplained circumstances. Who killed Vincent? Where is the money? How did you appear at my cottages?'

They had negotiated some traffic lights and a roundabout and were heading back the way they had come, with Amanda's sat nav making polite objections. Cat hardly noticed. She was more aware of the coldness of his tone. Previously and on occasion, that tone had been directed at her and chillingly so. Not this time.

She said, 'You don't like Amanda much, do you?'

He shrugged. 'It doesn't matter whether I like her or not. But I don't think I trust her.'

Cat knew her voice was hardly audible. 'She's my friend.'

'No doubt Lucretia Borgia had friends. Or Mata Hari. It doesn't mean you could trust them.'

Cat smiled in spite of herself.

'But I've always trusted her.'

Greg said gently, 'Perhaps because you're a nice person who generally sees the best in people.'

Cat didn't want to discuss this any more.

'What would you have done if Amanda hadn't forgotten the keys?' she asked.

And was that like Amanda? Perhaps sometimes she could have her head so filled with plans that she could be a bit absent-minded over the detail. But something this important?

'We would have run,' Greg said. 'And then found some other mode of transport. Hitched or something once we were out of sight. But no way am I going to ground again.'

Cat nodded and for the first time, noticed the trees flashing past the windows. 'Where are we going?' But she already knew the answer to that. 'And why?'

$$\star \quad \star \quad \star$$

As they left the shop, Amanda could hear Stephen muttering. She was trying to ignore him; he wasn't saying anything they hadn't discussed already. How many times did he need telling?

Belatedly picking upon her lack of concentration, he suddenly looked outwards, towards the pumps and beyond, to see what Amanda was looking at.

'Amanda! They've taken the car.'

She smiled slightly. 'Oh, dear, so they have.'

'But they're getting away.' He waved his arms above his head, as if that was going to make any difference. His arms dropped and he turned to face her. She was still smiling. 'You don't seem too bothered about it.'

'Don't I? Well, of course, stealing a car is a very serious matter. Particularly when it's mine.'

He was frowning. Amanda waited for the thought processes to work through. Almost as if she could actually hear them. He said, 'You must have left the keys in. That was risky.' He paused, then, 'You meant this to happen!'

'I wouldn't quite say that. But I thought it might. And please don't ask me where I think they're going, Stephen, because it's obvious.'

Stephen said nothing. Never mind. He would find out soon enough.

Amanda said, 'Phone call to make.' She pressed the required number.

Belatedly, Stephen got it. 'They'll kill them.'

'That would be their look-out, wouldn't

it?' Amanda murmured absently. 'And would save a lot of trouble all round. No, Stephen, don't look like that. I was joking.' Or was she? Maybe she wasn't quite sure about that herself. 'Anyway,' she said briskly, 'that's immaterial because for some reason, DB isn't answering. Really! You set people up with an amazing opportunity and they just can't manage to take advantage of it.'

'Have you the numbers for any of the others?'

She ignored that idiotic suggestion.

'I'll go for an alternative.'

'Ah. Who are you trying to get hold of now?'

'Someone who can arrange alternative transport for us if that's all right with you?'

Stephen grunted. 'Perhaps there will be no one in and Cat and Greg will come back again?'

'You never know. That could be an option.' And good; at least someone was answering her call.

★ ★ ★

This had to be Woodmere. A large house in red brick and fake Tudor style, with electric gates and a forbidding wall, surrounded by yet more trees. They had parked out of sight of the house, some way along the lane. The leaves seemed unnaturally still. The air was almost too hot to breathe.

'It doesn't look as if they welcome visitors,' Cat said. The trees cast dark shadows over the drive. 'Or the sunlight either.'

'It's better round the back. There's a private sun terrace — or there was.'

'You've been here before?'

'I came to a student party, years ago. Vincent's parents lived here, before they retired to Spain.'

'I see. Were they into criminal activities too?' She could understand why Greg had wanted to come here.

'It was hinted at sometimes. Vincent made a bit of a joke of it. I didn't take it seriously.' Greg paused. 'I don't think

Stephen did either. But who knows? Maybe he did. Maybe I was the only one believing the best of everyone.' He was looking up at the house, scanning the windows.

'So what now?'

'We go in. Maybe see what the Brystons have to say for themselves. And if they're not in, we may be able to find something useful.'

'We've already stolen Amanda's car and now we're going to be breaking and entering? Are you sure you've thought this through?'

Greg grinned. 'Perhaps not.'

'And if they are in — they think you've killed their brother and gone off with his share of the money in the business — and they know that you set fire to their SUV.'

'Not too good when you put it like that, I agree. Tell you what, shall we just forget it and go?'

'Do you really mean that?'

'Absolutely not.' Greg climbed out of the car. Cat followed as he pressed the buzzer by the gate. They waited. Cat's hands were cold and a shiver crossed the back of her neck.

A voice said, 'Yes?'

Greg lowered his voice. Cat smiled. It was a voice she had heard him use before. He said, 'Delivery for Bryston.'

There was a pause.

'We're not expecting anything.'

'Are you sure? I need a signature, mate.'

'This address is never used for deliveries.'

Greg paused. His face was pale. He said, 'Sorry, mate. I see now — the address is Woodmead. Sorry to trouble you.'

The voice from the speaker said, 'Or maybe I'm wrong. Hang on, I'll check. Won't take a minute.' In the background, they could hear another voice but not what was being said.

Greg said, 'No, definitely Woodmead. Sorry. I'm way out. Have to get on.' He pressed Cancel on the intercom.

Cat said, 'I don't get it. What are you

doing? He sounded as if he was going to let you in. Wasn't that what you wanted?'

'Back in the car. We need to get out of here.'

Cat obeyed. 'You look like you've seen a ghost,' she observed.

'Heard one, maybe.' He was starting up, driving further along the narrow lane, turning down a rough track and stopping once they were out of sight of the gate.

'Will they come out and check?'

'Probably. But I'm hoping they will assume we've gone back the way we came. That's the usual route.' He paused. 'Unless they have CCTV out here, but I don't think so. I couldn't see a camera, and Vincent never mentioned that when they had it put in. It's concentrated round the house.'

Distantly, they could hear the gates opening. Voices having a muttered discussion. The gates closing again.

'I didn't hear a car. So they're not going to look for us.'

Greg grinned at her. 'No. I think we've got away with it.'

'Let's face it, delivery drivers get things wrong all the time. Though we could have chucked a parcel over the gate, for extra realism.'

Greg laughed. 'Remind me to try that next time.'

'What now? Are we going to find the others?'

'We need to look round the back. It's a sunny day; there's a chance they'll be out on their terrace. Or some of them. Worth a try. We'll leave the car here for now. It isn't far.'

Cat followed, hoping there weren't any dogs. But she couldn't hear any barking. It seemed strange to her. If they wanted to find Greg so badly, why would the brothers be sitting out on a terrace enjoying the sunshine?

'This will do,' Greg said. 'I remember this wall crumbling a bit round here. We organised a booze delivery for the party through the gap.'

'Surely they'll have had it repaired?'

'Someone's made a half-hearted attempt. But that doesn't matter. We only need to look. Here, I'll give you a lift up. Don't let anyone see you.'

The wall was at least six feet high. Cat felt Greg hoisting her upwards; she clung onto rough hand holds and cautiously peered over the top. She looked down at Greg and nodded. There were three of them there. Two she recognised, and one she had never seen before.

Greg gestured that he was about to lower her. She murmured quietly into his ear what she had seen. 'I can have a go at lifting you. It's easy to hold on higher up.'

'Thanks, but I can't risk you dropping me. It would make too much noise.' He gazed round. 'Look, we can make a bit of a support with some fallen branches — and with you as well, I think that will be OK.'

Cat nodded. Silently and working with gestures wherever possible, they soon had a makeshift framework in place. Greg gave her a thumbs-up sign and began to climb, while Cat braced herself against the wood.

Being taller than she was, it didn't take Greg long. She listened, holding her breath. The terrace was not far away. If he stayed there much longer, surely someone would look up and see him?

At last, she felt the branches swaying under the strain as Greg began to make his way down. Supposing he slipped and fell? Supposing they heard him? No, he was standing beside her. He mouthed, 'Come on.'

She followed, silently but almost exploding with the unanswered questions. Even when they were back in the car, she said nothing, knowing he needed to concentrate on leaving as quietly as possible. Only when they had left the lane and rejoined the main road did she feel that it was safe to speak to him.

'Who did you see? Who was that third person?'

'That was Vincent.'

'What? It couldn't be.' Cat took in a deep breath. 'You mean, he's not dead?'

'No.'

It was a lot to take in. Cat felt as if everything had been turned upside down. 'But that means you're not wanted for murder. The police aren't interested in you. Oh, Greg, I'm so glad.'

'Yes, so am I — but I'll put my gladness on one side for now. Because why was I led to believe that he was dead — and for all this time?'

'You need to ask Stephen.'

'Yes, for starters.' He grinned at her. 'And that's where we're going now.'

Cat was thinking.

'But somebody obviously attacked Vincent — and you. Vincent may know who it was. We could have carried on with the delivery ploy after all and maybe found out.'

'If he knows, why would his brothers have been coming after me? Until I know more about their part in all this,

I'm steering clear.'

'I think it comes back to the money. Whoever attacked you both must have it — and that means Vincent doesn't know who it was.'

'But Stephen may?'

'Yes. So we'll go back to that garage where we last saw him and if they've moved on, we'll find that cottage Amanda was talking about. The sat nav will be only too happy to get back on track.'

'I could phone him and see where they are?'

Greg considered that. 'Not yet. That could scare him off. Let's keep him guessing for now.'

★   ★   ★

Stephen watched Amanda striding away from him. It could have been the automatic pacing everyone did when making calls — or she might be intending to keep her conversation private. Not much he could do about that, either way. He would just have to wait until she felt like sharing it with him. At least she seemed to know what she was doing. Knowing Amanda, she would have some plan in mind — if not several.

She ended her call but was continuing to stare at her phone, holding it at arm's length, her expression uncertain. Stephen was beginning to feel uneasy. Because it was so unlike Amanda to seem unsure of anything. He walked over to her.

'Everything OK?'

'Mmm? Oh, yes, fine. Why wouldn't it be? He'll be sending a car to pick us up shortly.'

'Who will?'

Amanda said, suddenly brisk, 'No problem. We can have a bite and a coffee while we wait.'

'Not that imminent, then?'

Again, she ignored his question. Stephen shrugged. No particular hurry, he supposed. And it wasn't his car that had been taken.

There was a queue in the Services cafe. He chose a sandwich pack without looking at it and heard himself ask for an Americano. Both could be snatched up and taken with him if necessary. Amanda had chosen a heated option — spag bol or something — and a salad. Obviously she wasn't expecting to leave before she had finished.

Stephen's unease was growing. He ate without tasting anything, his mind elsewhere. Rightly or wrongly and possibly for the most dubious motives — because he could see that now, he had fully intended marrying Cat — he had believed he was in love with her. Some of those intense feelings were still there, even though he now knew he had loved Amanda all along.

His own words were returning to haunt him. *They'll kill them.* And Amanda's flippant response. He was chewing and sipping as slowly as possible to try and occupy himself with something, anything — but at last the packet and cup were empty. It was no good. He couldn't take any more of this.

He mumbled something and went

over to the toilets. He couldn't just leave it and wait to find out what Amanda and this other person had in mind. He had to find out what was happening. He rang Cat's number.

For what seemed an eternity, there was no answer. He allowed it to ring and when Voicemail kicked in, he rang off and tried again. And again. His heart was thudding. What had happened to them? He groaned. This was all his fault. He should never have allowed Cat to get into this. He should have prevented it somehow. Though he had no idea what he could have done.

And at last, Cat answered. 'Hello, Stephen.'

He took a moment to register that she was actually speaking to him, sounding just the same as usual. 'Cat! Are you OK? Where are you?'

'No problem. We just made a small detour.'

He was still weak with relief. 'We guessed that. But what happened? Have they let you go? Are you both all right?'

He thought he heard Greg speak. Cat said, 'We never got in. So nothing happened at all.'

'Bit of a wasted trip for you, then.'

Cat hesitated. 'You could say that. But where are you now?'

'In the Services, where you left us.'

'That's good,' Cat said brightly. 'We can pick you up.'

Behind him, Amanda said, 'And return my car. Thanks.'

Stephen jumped. How long had she been there? And he wouldn't have expected her to follow him in here. He hadn't wanted Amanda to know he was going to try and contact Cat; she might have tried to stop him. However she didn't seem too worried that he had.

He said, 'We'll see you soon.'

★　★　★

Amanda was in the driving seat again, with Cat and Greg sitting meekly in the back. Cat thought, *Except that we know something now that changes everything.*

'Not far now,' Amanda said. They were driving through an endless residential area of red-brick and pebble-dashed semis. On to another dual carriageway. Turning off at last to pass through hedges enclosing flat, grassy fields and bumping down a little-used lane which became a track, edged with sand.

They seemed to be in the middle of nowhere. Sand dunes and marram grass and, way beyond, the murmuring sea.

'Here we are,' Amanda said, braking.

There was no sign of the cottage Cat had been imagining. She stared at the rambling structure in front of them.

'It's a shack.'

'That's why it isn't used now,' Amanda said. 'As I said, vulnerable to sand and sea.'

Greg said, 'Is it even habitable?'

'Oh, yes. It's fine. We're not going to be here long term.'

Cat caught a strange expression on Stephen's face as he glanced at Amanda. What did he know — or suspect?

Greg was saying, 'You're right. We're

not stopping long. It wouldn't be much use as a hiding place anyway. Too visible. Although it seems to have a roof, of sorts.'

'And what about the car?' Cat said. 'That will give us away.'

'Don't worry,' Amanda said. 'There are a couple of lean-to sheds at the side. They're bigger than they look. Give me a hand with the doors, someone.' She approached the nearer one.

The doors had a build-up of blown sand against them but once Greg and Stephen had kicked it away, they were pulled open without too much trouble. *Why go for that one?* Cat wondered. The doors on the other were clear. She supposed it didn't matter much.

Amanda drove the car in and joined them outside. Cat was staring round. Yes, this hut and the sheds would be visible for miles, in several directions. The only possible cover was provided by the surrounding sand dunes. At least she could be certain no one was observing them from a distance; no tell-tale glinting of sun on binoculars.

She could understand Greg's misgivings but surely they should be safe here for a while, enough to give them time to think things through and decide what to do next. And to observe Stephen's reaction to the news that Vincent was still alive. That would be interesting.

Amanda made a slight exclamation of annoyance and edged back through the door they had just pulled shut.

'Sorry, I've left something in the car. Here's the key, Greg. No, it's OK. You carry on. I'm just not quite sure where I put it.'

'This place actually has a key?' Greg sounded amused. 'Anyone could climb through that hole in the roof for starters. And the windows don't look up to much.' He unlocked the door; the key turned with ease. 'Hmm. I'm pleasantly surprised.'

Cat nodded. 'Someone must come and check it out regularly. That uncle Amanda mentioned, perhaps. Lucky for us.'

Had she heard Amanda talk about him before? She wasn't sure. She followed Greg inside. Stephen was a few steps behind her.

They stopped, looking round at the bare planks, the peeling paintwork, the dusty curtains. 'There's glass in some of the windows,' Cat said. 'That's good.'

There was a large main room, where the exposed roof joists were supported by four wooden posts, and a number of doors off.

'And furnished,' Greg added. 'Folding picnic chairs. What more do you want? Every bit as good as my cottage on the island.'

He tipped one chair, flicking sand off it.

Cat opened a door. 'This must be a bedroom. There are bunk beds and a mattress on the floor. The sand hasn't got in here.'

Stephen muttered, 'What about cooking? Where's the kitchen?'

'Yeah, that would be OK with sleeping bags,' Greg said. 'Maybe it's been let out fairly recently. Would be fine for bird watchers.'

'Cooking facilities?' Stephen said again.

Cat looked at him sharply. 'I doubt if there's even running water out here. Though you never know. We can get take-aways and sandwiches if we need to. Or manage with a camping stove. There may even be one somewhere.'

Greg was unfolding three of the chairs, placing them in a circle.

'Before we get onto that, Stephen, there's something we need to talk about.'

11

Stephen glanced around. *He looks hunted,* Cat thought, *and as if he's hoping Amanda will turn up and rescue him.*

And where was she? But all to the good if they could have this chat with Stephen on his own.

'Take a seat.' Greg was sitting down himself.

'What's this about?'

'Why did you tell me Vincent was dead?'

'What? What are you talking about? He *is* dead.' Stephen looked confused. 'We've been through this. I came in and saw Vincent on the floor, covered in blood and you were slumped against the wall. You staggered to your feet — and you had a knife in your hand and there was blood on you as well. And he was dead. He *looked* dead. I said, 'What have you done?' You looked down at yourself and at him and you said you didn't know. But you didn't deny it.'

'Didn't it occur to you that Greg could have been attacked too?' Cat asked. 'Why would he be slumped against a wall otherwise?'

'I didn't think he'd killed Vincent deliberately. I thought Greg had come to ask the very questions I wanted answering — and that Vincent had reacted badly and he and Greg had a fight. To be honest, my first thought was how lucky that I hadn't got there first or I would be the one bearing the brunt of it. And the outcome might have been very different; I might have come off worst — so when you arrived, Greg, you would have found *me* dead on the floor.'

'Never mind all that,' Greg said. 'You're just confusing things even more, with what might have happened and didn't.'

'The point is, I knew it looked very bad for you and I had to get you out of there.'

'I still don't see why you couldn't have left it to the police to sort out,' Cat broke in. 'Even if you were right about what happened, Greg would have had a good case for self-defence, surely?'

'But I was in shock,' Stephen protested. 'I was confused. It's no wonder you can't always make sense of my account because I don't feel I'm recalling everything accurately myself. Let's face it, Greg, I would have been a rubbish witness and made everything worse for you.'

Greg raised his brows.

'Pity you had so little confidence in yourself. Or me for that matter. You certainly managed to convince me I must be guilty.'

'I did think you were. You have to believe that. How could I put you through all that otherwise?' Stephen paused. 'Hang on. It sounds as if you don't think Vincent *is* dead.'

'Spot on. And that's because I know he isn't. Cat and I have just seen him. Not in too good a shape, even now, because he seems to need crutches. But he's very much alive.'

'I didn't know — I swear.' Stephen was alarmed. 'Did you speak to him? What did he say?'

'Only through the intercom. And he didn't know who I was. There's no need for you to worry about that. Yet. Although I'm wondering why you are looking worried about it?'

'Anything to do with that family is worrying. You never know what they're going to do next or how they'll react.'

Cat said, 'You thought Vincent, your friend, was dead and yet you just left him there?'

'No, of course not. I wouldn't do that. I phoned his brother — Dean. But I didn't tell him my name and I didn't use my own phone, I found a phone box.' He exhaled, shaking his head. 'Thank goodness, they must have got there in time. They must have taken him to A and E and maybe said he'd been in a fight or something. They must have come up with some story because they wouldn't want to involve the police, would they? Not if they didn't have to. They wouldn't want them poking around in their affairs and asking awkward questions.'

'Sounds plausible. I could almost believe you.'

Stephen hurried on. 'I know I said I'd tell you when I found anything out — but I meant if I found out who'd attacked him.' He paused. 'And you, of course. And I didn't find anything. So I didn't try to contact you.'

Cat was watching him with narrowed eyes. Was he telling the truth? Doubtful. There was a telltale sideways look he would often give when he wasn't. And now he was scratching one ear.

'You're lying,' she said.

'I think so too,' Greg said. 'But why? Why did you want me out of the way so badly? To give you time to get hold of the money since Vincent was out of the picture? — or you thought he was.'

'No! Not at all. I don't know what happened to the money. I've given up on it. Let the Brystons have it if they want it. And I'm certain that at least some of it is suspect anyhow. It's not worth the hassle.'

Cat shook her head. She didn't find that convincing. Not coming from Stephen.

Greg nodded. 'We'll leave that for now. What then, if not the money?'

Stephen shrugged.

'OK — it was because of Amanda.'

Simultaneously, Cat said, 'Amanda?' as Greg said, 'What's *she* got to do with it?'

Stephen looked from one to the other. As if trying to work out who would be the most sympathetic listener, Cat thought.

Stephen said, 'She's had her eye on you for a long time, Greg. She first spotted you at a party we all went to.'

'Are you sure?'

'Of course I'm sure. And I'll come clean, I didn't like it. I was jealous. No way was I going to let her get anywhere near you if I could stop it.'

Greg frowned. 'I never noticed.'

'I know,' Stephen muttered. 'Just as

well. When it seemed that Vincent was dead and you were implicated, I didn't stop to think — I just seized the opportunity to get you out of the way.'

Greg didn't seem to be listening to him.

'I had other things on my mind. I was already concerned about the way the business was heading. I didn't like it. Far too ruthless, with too many grey areas. My job was to seek out the young entrepreneurs for you, Stephen, to get their ideas off the ground. But some of the opportunities you found for them seemed to be provided by some very suspect characters.'

'That wasn't my fault.' Stephen's voice was sulky. 'I know the people you mean, but all those introductions came via Vincent. He was doing more than just handle the actual money.'

'And I was already seeking alternatives for myself, asking around about openings in the areas I really wanted. Conservation, ecology. I hadn't time to worry about relationships.'

Cat smiled sadly. No wonder, in the car, that Amanda had seemed annoyed when Greg had hardly seemed to remember her. A small burst of joy was erupting inside her. He hadn't noticed Amanda but he had noticed Cat, hadn't he? He had kept her out of danger, showed concern for her — however reluctantly to begin with. And he had kissed her.

No, she was getting carried away now. She didn't really know whether his kisses had meant anything or not. They could have been the result of the dangers they had faced together and he had been hoping to reassure her. Merely kindness. If only they could be something more.

Greg said abruptly, 'But Amanda ditched you anyway. And I was living on the island by then so I had nothing to do with that. And you had taken up with her best friend instead.'

Cat looked round. It had been very useful to have this chat with Stephen and on his own — but what was Amanda doing all this time? Was this

223

another of her plots?

Stephen stood up, sharply. 'I'm thirsty. I'm going to find the kitchen. See if there's water in the taps.'

Cat could hear the faint, tell-tale sound of his phone vibrating but he was making no move to answer it. And why did Stephen keep going on about the kitchen? She stood up too.

'We'll come with you,' she said firmly.

Once again, it was as if Greg was reading her thoughts as he nodded. 'We could all do with some water.'

There were only two doors they hadn't tried. 'This is a cupboard,' Greg said, peering round the first door. 'Has to be the other one. If there is one.'

Stephen's hand was twitching towards the phone in his pocket. Cat was watching him closely. 'I didn't know you were so domesticated. All this emphasis on kitchens. Never mind, if there aren't any facilities to speak of, we can just get sandwiches and takeaways as I suggested.'

'Too much coming and going,' Greg objected. His footsteps echoed on the wooden floor as he made for the last door. The sand on the planks was rough under Cat's feet.

She was right behind Greg and bumped into him as he stopped abruptly. He said, 'No!' and tried to bar her way with one arm, but she had already seen the man's body, crumpled on the floor with blood on his shirt. The knife on the floor beside him.

Cat had a moment of unreality. She blinked. She had imagined this scene so many times.

Greg was moving forward. Cat snapped out of it and darted after him as he was bending over the body. 'Don't touch him!'

Greg said, 'He may be alive. We can help him.'

'Yes, but I'll do it. Not you. Don't you see?'

She knelt down, trying to avoid the blood amid the sand on the floor. She was feeling for a pulse in the man's neck, listening for any slightest whisper of a breath. Knowing already that this time, it was indeed too late.

'He's dead. We mustn't touch the knife.'

Greg's voice was expressionless.

'It's one of the Brystons. I'm sure of it.'

And the one who had been the most ruthless. The one who had wanted to throw her over the cliff. Cat shuddered.

'Yes. But how did he get here?'

Greg straightened up. 'Also, I don't think the knife wound killed him — although it could have done. I think he's been shot. And where are the others?'

Cat looked round wildly as she stood up. 'They may be looking for him by now. Or perhaps they did this? Perhaps they had an argument, fell out amongst themselves.' She shook her head. 'Whatever happened, we have to call the police.'

Greg was already looking at his phone. 'No reception on mine. It probably kicks in on that track somewhere. How about yours?'

'What? Oh, I see.' She scrabbled in her pocket, her fingers suddenly clumsy.

She was shaking now. Easy to understand Greg's reaction when he'd found Vincent. She could hardly think straight.

'No. I haven't either. Perhaps we should go outside and see where we get something.'

'Too late,' Stephen said. Cat had forgotten about him. He was still standing in the main room, staring at the body, his face pale.

Cat said, 'Yes, I'm afraid it is. Too late for him. But we have to phone someone. Your phone's OK, isn't it? I heard it. Before.'

'That's not what I meant.' Stephen waved one arm towards the window and the track.

There was a vehicle outside, the tyres skidding on the sand. For Cat, time stopped. It was moving too fast and too slowly, all at once. Nothing made sense.

Car doors slamming, shadows across the floor, two dark figures appearing at the outer door. The Brystons were here.

And suddenly, Amanda's piercing scream cutting across all of it. She was pushing past the Brystons, her voice high and shrill. 'This is dreadful! We never meant this to happen. I didn't know they would kill him.' She was seizing Dean's arm. 'You must believe me.'

Cat stared at her, unable to speak. What was Amanda talking about? None of that had made any sense. Who did Amanda think had killed him? She stared at the two men. Dean's face was a mixture of grief and cold fury.

Greg said, 'We didn't kill him. We've only just found him. And what was he doing here, anyway?'

Dean said, 'Waiting for you. I should have thought that was obvious. But somehow, you got to him first. Well done. But unfortunately for you, you won't be enjoying your little triumph for too long.'

The second one said, 'You'll pay for this.' He was scowling.

Amazingly, Greg was remaining calm. 'If his job here was to — what — kill us? Or just to intimidate us? Whichever, you can hardly be surprised that he's ended up dead himself. Except that we had nothing to do with it. We've only just got here.'

'You're not going to believe that, are you?' Amanda cried. 'He's done it before and now he's done the same thing again.'

'Hardly,' Greg said. 'That doesn't make sense. What would killing him achieve for me? I want my innocence proved so I can get back to a normal life. I could hardly do that with a dead body. His or Vincent's. I wanted their evidence, not their deaths.'

Cat glanced at him. So he wasn't showing his hand as yet. Not revealing they already knew Vincent wasn't dead. She wondered why. Perhaps he was waiting for the right moment.

Dean shouted, 'Don't try and make a fool of me. You're after the money.'

'Am I? OK, Stephen and I shared in the work of making that money but I've had time to think things through over the last months. Money isn't every-thing.'

Dean gave a contemptuous snort.

'You can't expect me to believe that.'

Greg nodded thoughtfully.

'No, I probably don't. But it doesn't alter the truth. And money can never be worth a life.' He paused. 'Two lives now.'

'Easy for you to say when you're the one that has the money — ' Dean frowned. 'What do you mean, two lives?'

'I'm assuming you want me to believe Vincent is dead? And that you are acting as impromptu powers of attorney or something similar?'

Dean frowned.

'No. Why would we? You and your mate here rang us so we could pick him up.'

'Not me. I had nothing to do with that. I'd been attacked myself.'

The other Bryston brother pushed forward.

'You're not going to let this smooth talker worm his way out of it? That money's ours — and Vincent's. We're acting for Vincent. That's what you said. And now we're acting for Jimmy too. So whether this scum attacked Vincent or not, makes no difference. Someone's going to pay for killing Jimmy — and it might as well be him.'

Dean said, 'Shut up, Charlie. I'm thinking.' He turned to face Greg. 'OK, I'll go with you on that for now. Because the same argument works for us too. If you're dead, we're no nearer finding where the money is. No arguing, Charlie.' He addressed his brother without looking at him.

Charlie shrugged.

'Just say the word when you do want me to take steps. When you stop being clever.'

To Cat, the alliance between the two remaining brothers seemed dangerously fragile. Perhaps this could be used against them somehow? No need for her to try and point it out. She trusted Greg to work that out for himself.

And what was Amanda making of all this?

She glanced sideways to where Amanda was still standing in the outer doorway. The shock and horror she had demonstrated as she'd arrived — or a good attempt at those feelings — had now been replaced by an inappropriate expression of exhilaration.

Obviously she hadn't realised Cat was looking at her. Understandable, as the whole of Stephen's attention was focused on Greg and the Brystons — and Cat hadn't turned her head.

Now, left to herself, Amanda's expression changed again. She seemed annoyed and frustrated. Cat frowned, her eyes half closed. What was Amanda expecting to happen now? It looked as if she hadn't counted on Greg coming up with this argument; convincing Dean to regard him in a different light.

A great many differing fragments of information were falling into place.

Cat said suddenly, 'It was you, Amanda! You all along. You told the Brystons that you were bringing us here.'

That was why Amanda had pretended to be looking for something in the car — and why she had taken such a long time in her supposed search.

Amanda flashed her a look of anger. She began to shout over Cat, pulling at Dean's arm as she did so.

'Don't listen to her. Just do what you came here to do.'

Greg said quietly, 'And what would that be?'

Dean laughed.

'Yeah. Let's all hear this.'

Amanda shouted, 'Stephen, do something!'

As if he had abruptly become switched on by her words, Stephen made for the open kitchen window, shoving Cat and Greg out of the way, and began to climb through it.

Greg staggered against Cat and they both collided with one of the wooden posts. It seemed to wobble beneath Cat's shoulder. She looked upwards in alarm. How safe was it? No, there was no sign of the roof collapsing, in spite of the hole over her head. Not yet. She breathed a sigh of relief.

Dean said, 'Go,' and his brother Charlie was at once across the room, seizing Stephen and flooring him with a powerful punch to the jaw.

'That enough?'

'I would think so. He's only excess baggage, not capable of much. Keep an eye.' He turned to Amanda, who was still clutching his arm. 'After all, that's what you think of him, isn't it?' He turned to Greg. 'And I have to agree. I've been wasting my time trying to get anything out of him. He knows nothing. We've been on the wrong track all this time.'

He moved swiftly, clamping Amanda's hand. Cat could tell how much pressure he was exerting as Amanda winced.

She moaned. 'You're hurting me. Let me go.'

'Not just yet, darling. I think you've got it right, Cat. Where the money is now is nothing to do with any of the

234

original founders of the business at all. Because yes, Amanda did tell me she would be bringing you here. And I wasn't going to miss the opportunity. But I do wonder, Amanda, why you would do that?'

Greg was edging towards him.

'I agree with you on this. But we're not going to get at the truth by using violence.'

'Wimp,' Charlie Bryston muttered. 'Violence is the only way to get anywhere.'

'You're wrong,' Amanda said quickly. 'I don't know anything.'

Cat didn't understand any of this — and not for the first time. But Amanda had somehow got herself into a dangerous place and Cat had to help her.

She offered, urgently, 'You have to listen to her. Amanda's my best friend. We've been friends for years. She would never do anything to hurt me.'

Her brain was tumbling along as if of its own volition, because if it wasn't

Amanda who was responsible for all this, who could it be? Was it Stephen after all? Had he coerced Amanda into any involvement she'd had? It was obvious Amanda and Stephen were back together and should never have been apart. And yet, as he lay on the floor, still groaning and clutching his face, Amanda didn't seem too concerned about him.

In fact, Amanda seemed more worried about Cat. There was a sob in her voice as she said, 'I am your friend, Cat. I only want to help you.'

Dean laughed. 'Like you helped her at her hen party? When you wanted us to dump her somewhere? But I declined, if you remember. Because I couldn't see what the advantage for us might be. And I don't quite see what you hoped to gain from it, either — I doubt whether stopping the wedding was your motive because I'm not convinced you're bothered about that idiot on the floor there.' He sidestepped quickly, taking them all by surprise as he clamped an arm around

Amanda's neck. 'But you're going to tell us.'

Amanda shrieked, 'Help! Help me. Now.'

Cat felt as if she couldn't keep up. Whoever did Amanda expect to hear her, way out here among the dunes and the grasses?

Silhouetted against the lowering grey of the sky and a strangely sinister sunlight, a figure appeared at the open doorway. Cat's gaze went to his outstretched hand. The newcomer was holding a gun.

Her stomach contracted. Who was this?

Greg stepped forward.

'Mike! Good to see you. You've come just at the right time. But there's no need for that.' He gestured to the gun. 'We're just about to sit down and sort everything out.'

Cat shook her head in surprise. How could Greg seem so relaxed?

At once she realised her mistake. He wasn't relaxed at all. She could sense the tension he was striving to keep out of his voice.

But of course, this would be the Mike who had done so much to help them already — although usually out of sight. They owed him a lot.

Mike was shaking his head now.

'I'm afraid not. I didn't want to do this. But it looks like there's no help for it.'

12

Dean said sharply, 'It was you. You attacked Vincent — and now you've killed Jimmy.'

Mike's voice was slow and cool but Cat could see sweat gathering on his forehead. As her eyes adjusted to the light outside, she could see him more clearly. Dark hair and a neat dark beard. His eyes were flickering from one to the other of them, unable to rest.

The hand holding the gun seemed steady but Cat didn't think they could trust him to keep his cool. Whatever his intentions, a moment of panic might have him forgetting his original purpose and shooting around indiscriminately.

Mike said, 'Jimmy, yes. It was him or me. Easy, though. He really wasn't ready — and presumably he was here on his own to deal with whoever turned up? Just a real shame that all of you didn't arrive one at a time.'

He paused as if waiting for a response, but no one said anything. The shifting eyes were directed at the Bryston brothers now.

'All the same, I was still hoping that when you saw the body, you'd lose it and do the job for me.' He shook his head. 'That would have saved a lot of trouble.'

From the corner of her eye, Cat could see that Charlie was itching to respond to that taunting voice. What would be the best thing to do if he did? Dive for cover? And where?

Greg was speaking slowly and calmly, palms open. 'Come on, Mike. You're not making sense. What job would have been done for you?'

Mike made a contemptuous noise. 'You come on, Greg. Work it out. You're not stupid. Far too trusting, yes, but not stupid. And when I leave — '

'When *we* leave,' Amanda interrupted.

'Yeah, right. When we leave, it will

look as if it happened as I'd hoped in the first place. That you've all caught up with each other and taken your revenge — with sadly tragic results.'

'Meaning what, exactly?'

'Now you're just trying to distract me, Greg. Don't bother. Meaning, of course, that you will all be dead. Picture *The Gunfight at the OK Corral* crossed with the final scene from *Hamlet*.'

Cat gasped. How could this man admit it so casually? And why did he want to kill them all? And if so, why not get on with it instead of talking so much? Her brain was turning and twisting as she tried to think things through.

Ah, perhaps he was still after his original aim and trying to goad one or more of them into taking him on. In which case his actions might be justified as self-defence. She couldn't believe he would shoot them in cold blood.

But the Brystons might well have a go; there were two of them and they would assume they could rely on Greg and Cat not to interrupt. That made four against only one gun. Four plus Amanda . . . although Cat was no longer certain about her.

She realised that, without taking his attention from the group as a whole, Mike was focusing on her — and grinning. Creepily, as if he understood everything she had been thinking. Without looking at Cat's friend, he said, 'I've got a job for you, Amanda. That one — Jimmy, I believe, and now happily disposed of — also has a gun. He was the only one of the three to be armed. As he so obligingly told me during our little conversation when he thought he and I were on the same side. Because as planned, he came on ahead. All arranged.'

'By me,' Amanda interrupted. 'I arranged that.'

Mike nodded. 'I know — thanks. And I think he intended to take me out, hence the gun — but unfortunately for him, that didn't work too well. Just shove him to one side a bit, Amanda,

242

and you'll find that he's lying on it.' He paused as Amanda didn't move immediately. 'Are you sure you're up for this?'

Amanda said, 'Yes. Of course I am.'

Cat had never heard Amanda speak in this way before. She sounded like a different person altogether, cold and calculating. Cat couldn't help recalling Greg's words — it seemed like years ago — *Who needs friends like that?*

She said urgently, 'Amanda — why are you doing this?'

Amanda gave no sign of having heard her. She was following Mike's instructions, finding the other gun with no sign of reluctance now. She picked it up, pointing it at the others as she crossed the room to stand by Mike.

Cat said, 'I'm so sorry if it's all about Stephen. But you had dumped him already — and he was so upset. I thought you'd accepted that.'

Amanda's face changed as she sneered.

'And you can't bear people to be

upset, can you, Cat? You just have to make everything better. You can't help yourself. Of course he was upset. I meant him to be. He wouldn't tell me anything. He was holding out on me. I wanted to show him I would come back and be part of his life, but only on my terms. If he agreed to share the secret with me.'

'What secret?' Cat was lost once more.

'She means the money,' Greg said. 'That's what this is all about for her. Always has been.'

Now Amanda had started, however, it seemed she didn't know how to stop.

'I had it all planned out. But then you came along interfering. Sweet little Cat. So ready to pick up the pieces and console him with a whirlwind romance. It was all so easy for you.' The gun shook in her hand, and she gripped it in both.

'It's always been easy for you. School, uni, work, loving parents. Everything you wanted, you only had to click your fingers and it fell into your lap.'

'But we were friends. Always, through everything. Weren't we?'

'That's what you always said. I just followed along behind, sometimes being lucky enough to share in the light of your success. Sometimes you would even put in a good word for me. Recommend me for a job every so often. When you felt like it.'

Cat felt ripped apart. How could she have got this so wrong? Surely there must have been something between them?

'I've always done my best to support you. From when we were quite small and yes, you had all that trouble with your family. Don't you remember?'

'Oh, yes. I certainly do. And stupidly, I appreciated the help at the time. My mum and dad always rowing, and when he walked out — I didn't know why. And my mum was in pieces but when I wanted a safe haven, I always came round to yours. Where everything seemed calm and normal and I was always welcome.'

She gave Cat a look of complete disgust. 'I can't believe it. You still don't know, do you?'

Cat's heart was thudding. She didn't want to hear this but she heard herself asking all the same. 'Know what?'

Amanda screamed at her.

'That my dad walked out because he discovered your father was having an affair with my mum. That's when it all blew up — but then apparently your father wasn't too serious about it. Wrecked our lives, and then was all penitent and remorseful. Your mother let him stay.'

Cat felt the colour draining from her face. She whispered, 'I can't believe it.' While knowing that she did. It made sense of so many little things.

Greg said, 'Be quiet, Amanda. Cat doesn't need to hear this.'

A small part of Cat was grateful for that. But she shook her head.

'No, it's all right. I need to know.' She looked Amanda straight in the face, unflinching. 'When did you find out?'

'Oh, about five years ago. When your mother died. That's when my mum told me. And you know what, I decided not to tell you. To let you remain happily in ignorance. Because what would be the point?' Her voice was scornful. 'And because not long after that, I'd heard of this trio of entrepreneurs at uni and I saw the potential in their online business; I decided if I played my cards right, I could be a part of that, one way or another. And it would be a kind of compensation for the rough deal I'd been handed by life.'

Above Stephen's head, the opened window banged against the wall, caught by a stray gust of wind. Below it, Stephen was pulling himself up. He mumbled, 'I don't have the money.'

'No,' Amanda said contemptuously. 'I know that now. I was wasting my time bothering with you, from the first. But you'd seemed the easiest to move in on. And I thought you would be the best bet for telling me what I wanted to know. When it didn't turn out that way and you took up with Cat — ' She shrugged her shoulders in what was obviously self-disgust. 'I should just have left you to it, two losers together, instead of trying to keep you apart.' She tossed her hair back. 'Not to worry, it's all going to work out now. Perhaps it's better this way. Getting rid of all the obstacles in my way at once and beginning afresh.'

Cat felt once again that she was living in a nightmare. She looked over at Mike. He was actually grinning, as if he was enjoying himself. And yet the expression in his eyes was like nothing Cat had ever experienced — cold and utterly ruthless. For the first time, she understood what Amanda had meant. Now Cat believed in Mike's intentions. He was going to kill them all. None of them would leave here alive.

But it seemed Mike was revelling in his control of the situation.

'No one else with something to say?' He paused. 'How about you, Greg?'

Cat realised Greg must also be feeling betrayed but he was succeeding in keeping his face blank.

'What is there to say? I thought you were helping me out of a difficult situation because of our long friendship. Obviously I was wrong, too.'

Mike was crowing now. 'Did you never wonder why I should go to so much trouble? Providing somewhere for you to hide so you didn't need to go to the police? Giving you everything you needed when your hiding place was so unfortunately discovered and you had to run again. Vehicles, money, everything. You only had to ask.'

'Yes. That's what friends are for. I would have done the same for you.'

'I'm sure.'

'But how was it our friends here found the island and the cottages? And how did Cat come to be there?'

'That's an interesting question,' Dean interrupted. 'I was wondering that myself. Although I can answer the first part of it. Amanda approached us,

249

wanting to rope us in to remove Cat for her. She's very plausible when she wants to be. And just throwing in as a casual aside that the island was a conservation area with a warden I might have heard of, just happening to mention his name.

'Two things we wanted, both at once. The man who had attacked Vincent and who was one of my suspects for knowing where the money had gone. And yet — now she had told us the locations, why should we get ourselves in trouble for abducting a girl with nothing to do with it? Something didn't seem quite right. And there was nothing in that part of it for us. So I declined. But obviously the next person she tried accepted.' His voice and manner were totally calm.

Cat thought, *What was it Stephen had been told? That I left the hen night with a man with a beard? Mike has a beard. I should have remembered that from when he had given them the old Land Rover. But so many people have beards these days.*

Dean, Greg and Mike were standing as if in a triangle, staring at each other. Who would break eye contact first? Cat's eyes slid to Charlie Bryston, who was anything but calm. If she had thought he was in a dangerous mood before, that was intensified now. His whole body was tense, his eyes flickering back and forth — to Mike and Amanda and the guns, to Greg, to his brother. She hoped Mike hadn't noticed.

Idiot, she told herself, of course he had noticed. This was exactly what he had been waiting for.

She must try to think of something to distract him. But her thoughts would insist on following their own paths. Because, good grief, how many strands were entangled in this plot? How long had Amanda been planning her aspects of it?

At least Cat now knew why — and would have to try and think about that later, and her father's part in it, if they ever escaped from this mess.

And Mike too — and at what point had he and Amanda come together to form such a toxic partnership?

She tried to scan Mike's face, trying to read his thoughts. He was still standing in the open doorway, with Amanda to one side of him, silhouetted against the ever darkening slate-grey of the sky. It was far too dark for this time of day. What was happening?

But if she couldn't see Mike's face clearly, perhaps that meant that he couldn't see Charlie either, through the increasing gloom.

Into the silence, Greg said, 'You haven't answered me, Mike. Why?'

Mike said nothing. Was he even intending to answer? It seemed that he was struggling now to maintain the calm stance. When he spoke, his voice was intense, his words clipped.

'And you can pretend you don't know?'

'I wouldn't ask, would I? Shall I guess? Maybe it was you who attacked Vincent — but I suspect you thought

252

you'd killed him, as you hoped. And helping me to hide covered it up for you. But that still doesn't tell me why you did any of this.'

Was Greg also trying to goad Mike into making a mistake? A dangerous tactic. But Cat felt she could trust Greg to get this right. And otherwise, they seemed to have reached a stalemate.

There was a sudden burst of movement as Charlie lunged rashly across the space between him and Mike.

Mike fired, twice, and Bryston slumped to the floor, crashing against the weakened post as he fell. Cat stared at him in horror. She had forgotten to keep watching him. Still, how could she have stopped him?

Whatever had he been thinking of? Perhaps he was tired of waiting. Perhaps he had assumed Mike was distracted by Greg. Whatever had driven him, he had made a desperate mistake.

Into the silence, Mike said, 'OK, two down and three to go. Who's next?'

Dean remained calm.

'So obviously it was you who attacked Vincent and stole his laptop. And our money.' His voice was ice cold.

'Of course I did. I don't know why you were all so slow on the uptake.'

'And obvious too that you have the money,' Greg added. 'I'm right on that? But I still don't understand why.'

'Correct.' Mike gave a harsh laugh. 'Why don't you try and guess? You'll never get there. You're just too dumb. You've blocked it all out.'

Was Charlie dead? Cat thought. No one seemed too worried about finding out — even Dean. They were all ignoring him as he lay on the sand and planks at their feet. They should call for an ambulance. Not that Mike would allow that.

Dean said, 'I'm interested to know too. Who's blocked what out?'

Mike made an impatient noise. 'How it all started. And Vincent was just as guilty of this as these other two. Oh, yes. It was all my idea. Your brilliant business venture. I thought of it.' His face was

254

transformed into an ugly scowl. 'You've forgotten all about that, haven't you?'

Stephen grunted something. It could have been, 'No,' but when Mike glared at him, he shook his head.

Greg said, 'I'm sure we all remember the circumstances very well. You got into debt when we were at uni — and to some pretty undesirable people as I recall. I seem to remember an incident of your door being kicked in. You were scared witless and that was all you could think about, how to get some money to repay the debt. So you told us about your idea and offered to sell somebody, anybody, a share in your embryonic business. We all thought it was a great idea. And when Vincent and Stephen offered to buy you out, you leaped at it. They wanted complete control, not just a share — or not with you. And I went in with them. Between us, we got you off the hook.'

'It wasn't fair!' Mike shouted. 'You could see I was desperate. You took advantage of me. That initial debt of mine was tiny compared with the amount you've all made since.'

'We took a risk.' Greg's voice was mild. 'We didn't know whether it would succeed. I half thought I'd never see my money again — but I wanted to help you out. And there was no way we could have allowed you to stay a part of the business. Not with your gambling habit and the mess you'd got yourself into. It could just as easily have happened again. Apart from that, however, I had no idea this was how you felt. Why didn't you get back to us and try to renegotiate?'

Mike gave a wild laugh. 'Oh, I did. But I got it wrong, didn't I? Thought I'd save time by going to the main man, the one it was obvious was calling all the shots. A big mistake. I should have tried you, shouldn't I? The decent one, the soft touch.'

Greg's voice was deceptively quiet.

'But you went to Vincent instead.'

'Of course I did.'

Cat couldn't take her eyes from the

gun. Mike was obviously losing it — and if only he would lose his concentration too, there might be a chance of the others trying to overpower him. But no, in spite of the telltale variations in his voice, his hand remained steady.

'And what happened then? Or need I ask? You attacked Vincent.'

'It wasn't like that. I was perfectly calm and reasonable, explaining what I wanted. I made a good case. And do you know what? He laughed in my face.' His face was contorted with anger. 'I saw red. Can you blame me? I shoved him and he fell. He banged his head on something and lost conscious-ness. And I realised how easy it would be, to take him out altogether and nick his laptop while I was about it. I got a kitchen knife but I'd hardly started with it when you turned up, Greg. I heard you on the stairs before you'd had a chance to see anything so I knocked you out as you came through the door and put the knife in your hand. And went.'

'And presumably Stephen wasn't far behind.'

Mike shrugged. 'I didn't wait to find out. Although it seems Stephen had his own ideas on all this and decided to implicate Greg even more.'

Cat could stay quiet no longer.

'Why bring Greg into this at all? Presumably you had the money once you'd left, hacking into the accounts somehow. Why not just take off to Spain or somewhere?'

Mike nodded, eyes half-closed.

'It was tempting but nothing's ever that simple. I wasn't going to risk leaving any kind of trail, leading back to me. Not when I'd found out about Vincent's calibre of relative. Better to help Greg escape, reinforcing his guilt.'

Dean said, 'And every so often dropping us a hint to lead us straight to him.'

Amanda interrupted, 'That was me.'

Mike ignored her. He was still looking at Dean.

'I overestimated you three. I thought

you'd be after straightforward revenge, instead of getting hung up on who had the money. And wasting time and energy trying to get these two to tell you where it was. And of course, as long as they refused to tell you, they were safe. I slipped up there. But no worries, I can put that right now. Nothing's going to stop me.' He laughed again. 'And then I can settle back and enjoy my money.'

'We can,' Amanda said.

'What?' Mike shrugged. 'Yes, of course.'

Suddenly Cat knew what to do.

'Don't trust him, Amanda. Why ever are you joining up with him? He's obviously very dangerous and he's using you. Can't you see that? And he'll drop you as soon as he can.'

If she could only weaken Amanda's allegiance to him, that might help.

Amanda shouted, 'Shut up. That's just what I'd expect you to say. You know nothing at all about it, or our feelings for each other. You're just jealous, as usual. You have to take everything of mine for yourself. Like your father, wrecking our lives. Grab, grab, grab. Well, it stops here.'

Mike was laughing openly at her now. 'It's OK, Amanda. I'm moved by your loyalty but I think we can leave Cat for now.'

There was no stopping Amanda. She kept going. Cat was hardly listening, because it was obvious Mike wasn't. And what was he going to do next? She didn't like the way he was looking at her.

She glanced sideways to see whether Greg had noticed and how he was reacting — and realised that Greg, behind his back, was making small signalling movements with one hand. Was he signalling to her — and if so what did he mean?

It took a huge effort of will for Cat not to respond in any way, although she was itching to look round to see who else might be able to see what he was doing.

She bent quickly as if to knock an

insect from her knee. Stephen? No. He was still slumped against the wall, gingerly stroking his jaw. Ah, now she had it. Dean also had a hand behind his back and was making similar movements. They were evidently trying to communicate something to each other.

There was no time to watch more closely and work out what they were trying to do. The best way she could help was to trust that Greg knew what he was doing, and try to keep Mike and Amanda distracted.

She opened her arms wide, palms open in what she hoped would seem a peace-making gesture — while blocking Mike's view of Greg at the same time. Her voice wobbled.

'This isn't you, Amanda. Not after all those years of friendship when we meant so much to each other. It was a genuine friendship, you know it was. You've obviously been under a lot of strain since finding out about my father and I'm so sorry for that. I had no idea.

'I've been at fault in not realising

how you were feeling over the last few months. I was so stupidly wrapped up in what I thought was my new romance — and I can't apologise enough for that too. It was a huge mistake. I shall always regret it.' She tried to keep her voice gentle which wasn't easy with all the tension she was feeling. 'This isn't you. You don't go round shooting people. You've been a wonderful friend, warm and caring, and always ready to listen.'

'More fool me.'

'Come on, Amanda. Put the gun down.' Slowly, Cat took another step forward. And another. There seemed to be an expression of doubt crossing Amanda's face. Had she done it? Was Amanda listening?

It was so dark now that they could hardly see. Surely it wasn't that late? It was disorientating. And using herself as a makeshift screen was hardly necessary. Cat had to screw her eyes up to see Amanda's face although she was very close to her now.

Mike said, almost lazily and obviously in control of himself once more, 'I didn't think you would be so easily swayed, Amanda.'

Amanda's voice was unaturally high.

'I'm not. Don't even think it.' She waved the gun wildly. 'Get back, Cat, or I will shoot — '

The storm hit.

13

The wind gusted through the open door, sweeping through the window Stephen had left swinging wide. It was tearing through the hole in the roof, snatching at the corrugated iron sheeting. It was blinding them with the gritty, choking cloud of sand that it brought with it.

With a horrendous creaking and groaning, the roof joists caved in. Cat, Greg and Dean were already moving. It was as if they had been able to discuss what they were going to do as they took advantage of this surprise.

Greg dived towards Mike as the doorframe above him collapsed, taking Mike down with it into a tangle of splintered wood.

Dean went for Mike's gun as it flew out of his hand. Cat threw herself at Amanda, focussing on the arm that was holding her weapon.

Amanda screamed in fury as she fell while Cat lunged at that gun as it slid across the floor — and missed. She was dimly aware of somebody reaching for it and hoped it was Greg, but she was too preoccupied now with Amanda. Throwing all her weight on her friend as she tried to restrain her, she panted, 'Keep still. I don't want to hurt you.'

'That's right,' Dean sneered. 'Stop screaming, sweetheart. The situation just reversed itself.'

Amanda subsided, glancing over at the silent Mike. Greg was slowly standing up as if there was no need to keep him down. As suddenly as it had arrived, the wind subsided.

Cat said, 'Is he OK? He isn't dead, is he?'

'No, he's breathing. Just knocked out for now.' Greg gestured to the planks over Mike's legs and body. 'But I don't think he'll be going anywhere when he comes round.' He turned to Dean. 'We need to send for an ambulance. And not just for him. He can't stop us now.'

Dean nodded.

'I expect we do. And we will. But not yet.'

'Meaning?' Greg's voice was calm. Cat could hardly believe how calm he seemed. No one would think he was talking to a firearm in an outstretched hand.

And where was the other gun?

'I would have thought it was obvious. Bring him round. Tap his face a bit. Rough him up, even. We need to know where our money is.'

'That may be the way you do things,' Greg answered, 'but it isn't mine.'

'We're not messing about.' Dean was becoming angry now. 'Do it.'

Greg gestured to the splintered wood heap. 'You can see how his legs are trapped. I'll shift some of this wood — and if the pain of that brings him round, so be it. But I'm not going to try and hurt him any more than necessary.'

Cat shifted her weight on Amanda, wanting to go and help, but Amanda must have sensed her movement; she was obviously bracing herself to try something. Cat pushed her back.

Dean snarled, 'Get on with it, then.'

Greg obeyed, panting with the exertion.

'No point rushing it. Unless you want him to be too injured to talk at all.'

Dean grunted. Greg shifted a heavy plank to one side. As it fell with a crash, Mike groaned.

'What's happening? What are you doing?'

'Getting you out of this,' Greg answered. 'Keep still.'

Mike's face was pale, his lips bloodless.

'I think my legs are broken.'

Dean snapped, 'We're not interested in your legs. What have you done with the money?'

Dazed and blinking, Mike turned his head to see who was speaking.

'You expect me to tell you? Just like that? No chance.'

'You know the alternative,' Dean said.

Mike attempted a laugh.

'I don't think so. There's no point in threatening me. Kill me and you'll never find it. But help me out of this lot — and I may be willing to give you a share.'

'We're not here to make a bargain. I don't have to shoot to kill, do I? The injuries you've suffered already will be nothing, trust me.'

Mike blanched.

'Try me,' he croaked, seemingly unaware of how much the fear in his eyes was betraying him.

'Don't worry, I shall. And don't forget your girlfriend here. Are you happy to watch me putting a bullet or two into her, doing nothing to stop me?'

Mike tried to shrug and winced.

'Do what you like to her. It's not as if she matters much to me.'

Cat could sense the fury bubbling within Amanda; she could hardly hold her. Was Amanda wanting to attack Mike?

Greg said, 'There's no need for this.'

'No,' Amanda cried. 'No need at all — because I know where it is. Or how to get at it. I know his password and security details. Include me when you're sharing it out and I'll show you.'

'She's bluffing,' Mike shouted. 'She can't know.' He turned his head wildly, grimacing with pain. 'Don't believe what they're saying. Don't do this to try and save me.'

'Save you?' Amanda's laugh was harsh. 'Why would I do that? And yes, I do know. You've been very careless with your security. You underestimated me all along. You just never realised how much. And since you're not bothered what Dean here might do to me and you've obviously never cared about me, I might as well say I've never cared about you either.'

Mike swore. 'No. You can't do this.'

'I joined up with you because I thought you would be useful. I always knew that was your motive, too.' She turned to look at Cat, who was still sitting on her legs. 'Let me get my phone out, Cat, and I'll show you all what I can do.'

Cat frowned. Could they trust her? She no longer felt that she knew Amanda or anything about her. She glanced at Greg who half-shrugged and nodded. What had they got to lose?

Dean snapped, 'I'm losing patience here. You'd better not be messing us about.'

'I wouldn't do that.' Amanda was calm now.

'Get on with it, then.'

Amanda was reaching behind her for her bag, still slung around her shoulder. Cat shifted and moved the bag round. Amanda winced.

'You're hurt too,' Cat said.

'Just some bruising.' Amanda was delving in her bag now.

'Wait.' Dean commanded. 'Give the phone to Cat. Let her do it.'

Amanda shook her head, wincing again.

'No, I have to do it myself.'

'Say them out loud as you do it.'

'Oh, no. That would be far too easy. I would be giving all my cards away.'

'You don't have any cards. You're in no position to argue.' Dean waved the gun in Amanda's direction.

'But that's exactly what I am. Think about it. You've been in this position before. Kill me and there's no way you'll ever get the money back. I'm being very reasonable. All I want is a sensible share.'

'You've no right to it anyhow,' Dean growled. 'Less right than anyone else here.'

'Wrong,' Amanda said. 'I have the right of possession.' With her phone in her hand, she began moving her fingers, swiftly and surely.

Cat was holding her breath. No doubt Amanda's courage was driven by desperation and greed but she was brave — and foolhardy.

Mike shouted, 'No!' He was trying to pull himself across the debris. It was evident that his legs, although no longer trapped, wouldn't obey him. He grasped a piece of loose wood, stretched over to Amanda and tried to knock the phone out of her hand.

'That's enough of that,' Dean said. 'Greg? Stop him.'

But Greg was already moving, pulling Mike back, and none too gently as Mike tried to swing the wood at his head. Quickly, Greg kicked it out of his grip and across the floor.

'Too late,' Amanda said. 'I'm in. Looks like there's plenty for everyone. Here, Dean, come over and get it.' She waved the phone in Dean's direction — but nowhere near enough for him to reach it without coming close to her and Cat.

'No,' Dean said. 'I'm staying here. Give the phone to Cat. Take it in one hand, Cat and toss it over to me.'

'Right,' Cat said meekly. 'Help me hold her, Greg.' And as Dean seemed about to object, she added, 'We don't want her trying anything, do we?' It should have been obvious that her hold on Amanda was tenuous. She wasn't exaggerating.

She moved round as Greg joined her

272

and for the first time, she could see beyond Dean and appreciate the extent of the damage the storm had done to the rest of the building.

Greg said, 'You keep hold of her and pass it to me.'

As Dean made an impatient noise and was saying, 'No need for that. Just get on with it,' Cat had already reacted. She tossed the phone carefully to Greg who in the same movement, threw it strongly and directly into the centre of the tangled heap of splintered wood behind them.

Cat gasped — it could so easily have rebounded and landed at Dean's feet, but no. Greg's aim was accurate and the phone slipped through a convenient hole to disappear inside.

Swearing, Dean turned and dived after it, tearing at the broken planks blocking his way.

'Run,' Greg muttered urgently, grabbing Cat's hand. 'Leave her.'

Cat didn't argue, understanding what he was trying to do as she followed him through what had once been the doorway.

'Where are we going?'

Dean wouldn't be distracted for long. Her heart sank as she glanced across the bleak surrounding dunes. If anything, the hillocks seemed lower than before. The wind seemed to be rising again in small treacherous gusts and she had to half close her eyes against the blowing sand.

Even so, whichever direction they took, Dean would have no trouble in following them, if he chose. The all-terrain vehicle in which the Bryston brothers had arrived was standing outside.

'Garage,' Greg said, taking her hand.

Yes — there was more than one ramshackle shed serving that purpose. Amanda's car was in there, of course — and no doubt Mike had driven here too. Luckily the shed door was facing against the wind and had not yet come to any harm.

She began to help Greg pull the doors open, hoping the wind would keep off until they had got one of the vehicles out.

'We need Mike's keys,' she gasped as she heaved. Somehow Mike had squeezed his vehicle in behind Amanda's; she hoped they would be able to manoeuvre it out.

Behind them, Amanda said, 'No need. I have mine.'

Cat turned sharply. Amanda's footsteps had been cushioned by the sand and the noise of the wind as it blew round the doors. She was showing no sign of any injuries.

Cat said, 'I thought you were hurt.'

'No. Hard luck. And I'm coming too.'

Greg shrugged. 'Do what you like. Cat and I aren't going anywhere.'

'We're not?' For once, Cat hadn't been able to work out what he was planning.

'Think about it. He'll chase after us in his or Mike's and the whole thing will start up all over again.'

'But if he has the money, why would he bother?'

'Because he'll never believe we don't

want it; he'll only feel safe when he's got rid of us.'

Cat nodded. 'Yes, of course.'

'You go if you want, Amanda. I won't stop you. When he comes out here after us, we can trap him somehow, take him by surprise — and then get the police here.'

'Absolutely.' Cat agreed. 'Let them sort it all out.' At last. Her limbs felt weak with the relief of that prospect.

'That's a stupid idea,' Amanda said. 'No way am I waiting here.' She got into her car and tried to start it. But even within the comparative shelter of the garage, more sand had got in than might have been thought possible. The engine spluttered and the wheels simply spun.

Greg was leading the way to the back of the shed.

'She can't go,' Cat said.

'Doesn't matter much either way. Dean will come out to try and stop her — or us, as he thinks. And that's what we want.'

Cat tilted her head. 'I can hear someone shouting. Sounds like he's found the phone.'

Amanda was desperately trying the engine again. Now she was screaming in frustration — at the car, the sand — it was difficult to make out her exact words. She opened her car door and shouted through the gap. 'Push me.'

Cat said doubtfully, 'We can try.'

'Better still,' Greg said. 'We'll use the Land Rover to push.' He felt in his pocket and produced Mike's keys.

'How — ?' Cat began. Oh, yes. Mike had loaned it to them. It seemed like days ago.

'He gave me his spare set. I still have them,' Greg announced, with a grim smile.

'Get on with it!' Amanda shrieked.

Cat glanced round. Was that more shouting she could hear? Why was Dean not running straight out here? What could be holding him up?

Oh, of course. It must be Stephen. Stephen? That didn't seem likely. And yet from the corner of her eye she had seen someone pick up Amanda's gun. It must have been him. Although she didn't have much confidence in Stephen delaying Dean Bryston for long.

She scrambled into the passenger seat where next to her, Greg was already starting up. She said anxiously, 'The wind's coming back.'

'Thought it would. Eye of the storm. Don't worry. We'll be OK driving this.'

With a jolt, the Land Rover moved forward, bumping gently into Amanda's car. Greg had judged it perfectly. Amanda was simultaneously trying her keys again and the small car whined, roared and shot out of the garage at speed. At the same moment Dean appeared in the entrance.

There was a sickening thud and Cat had a dizzying impression of his body flying upwards, landing on Amanda's bonnet and bouncing off again.

Greg jammed on their brakes. Cat screamed, 'Amanda, stop!'

She thought at first that Amanda

would ignore her — but having gained the secure ground of the concrete track, Amanda did stop. She leaped out of the car, stooped over Dean's body, picked something up and was off again. Back in the car and away up the track, cleared of sand for now by the wind.

Cat said, stunned, 'She's taken his gun.' There was a tightening feeling of horror in her chest.

Greg leaped out of the Land Rover and ran to where Dean was lying, twisted at an unnatural angle. Cat thought he must already be dead but no, there was a faint pulse in his neck. He opened his eyes. Cat could hardly hear him. He gasped, 'She's got that phone.'

Cat said, 'You need an ambulance.'

Greg was talking into his phone. 'I've got reception out here.' He bent his head, speaking into the wind. 'That's OK, they're on their way.'

'No.' Dean gathered all his strength to shout. 'Don't bother with that. Get after her. Take mine. Four wheel drive.

No problem in sand.'

'Give me the keys,' Cat demanded. 'And you'd better be right.' She couldn't believe how calm and controlled her voice sounded when that wasn't how she was feeling. Her legs were almost giving way as the colour drained from her face.

'Let her go,' Greg said. 'The money doesn't matter. It's caused enough trouble.'

Dean groaned, but Cat ignored him. She snatched the keys from Greg's hand.

'I have to stop her. I know where she's going.'

14

'You can stay here and wait for the ambulance,' Cat instructed Greg.

At last Greg had sensed the urgency of what she knew.

'What? No chance. Not when she has the gun.' He leaped into the passenger seat as Cat set off. She was accelerating past the ruins of the buildings when a figure, waving his arms wildly, jumped out in front of her. She braked sharply in a shower of sand.

Stephen. Cat shouted, 'Get out of the way.'

'I'm coming with you.'

Greg snapped, 'We don't need you. Wait here for the emergency services.'

Stephen was still waving his arms and shaking his head. 'I can help you. She'll listen to me.'

'Get in,' Cat screamed. They didn't have time to argue, although she didn't think he would be much use. And if she couldn't get going again on the volatile surface, she would never forgive him.

He fell into the back.

'I don't see why I should help the medics find that lot. They wouldn't do that for us.'

'It's OK.' Greg placed a reassuring hand briefly on Cat's arm. 'We'll sort this.' He turned. 'What are you doing, Stephen? You'd better not be ringing Amanda. Give me that phone.'

'I wasn't.' Stephen sounded indignant. But he passed the phone over without any further argument.

Cat set off, exhaling with relief. She had to concentrate on driving the unfamiliar vehicle but at least it responded well, even in these hostile conditions. Only the best for the Bryston brothers.

'She's getting ahead.' Stephen sounded frantic. 'We're losing her.'

'And whose fault is that,' Greg scoffed, 'jumping out at us like that?'

Cat ignored them both because losing sight of Amanda didn't matter. If she had this right, she knew only too well where Amanda was heading — and what she intended. And if she was wrong, she didn't care where Amanda ended up. She hoped against all hope that she was wrong . . . but was horribly certain she was not.

'I think she was bluffing,' Stephen said. 'I don't think she can get into that account. But that doesn't matter because I have a plan that will solve that.' In spite of his concern about Amanda getting away, he sounded pleased with himself.

Greg turned to face him.

'Stephen, will you get it into your head that I'm not interested in the money? And therefore, not in what Amanda chooses to do with it. How many times do you need to hear it? You and I both had concerns about the way the business was going. That was why we went to see Vincent that day. His brothers had had far too much to do with it. It's easy to see that now.'

'They shouldn't have,' Stephen objected.

'It was us three who were doing all the work.'

'Of course. But we took a regular salary, didn't we? A good one. We were stupid, Stephen. We should have realised no way could a new, young business pay us like that. But we both concentrated on what we were doing and left all the financial side to Vincent and we shouldn't have done. You know this.'

Cat was allowing the discussion to go on somewhere above her head as if it had nothing at all to do with her. She couldn't afford to be distracted. She didn't even have time to set the sat nav, but fortunately she didn't need to. Once back to that motorway they'd used to get here, she knew the way.

Greg said, 'Shut up, Stephen. None of this is important. Cat, where are we going — and why?'

Cat took a deep breath.

'She's taken the gun — and I think she's going to try and shoot my dad.'

'What?' Stephen shouted. 'That's

284

ridiculous! She wouldn't. And why should she?'

'Revenge.' Cat made herself speak slowly and carefully. 'You heard what she said.' She still hadn't had time to process what Amanda had revealed about their parents. She wasn't sure she wanted to. When she did, she would be no use at all to anyone for — what, days, weeks? If she ever managed to get over it at all. She didn't know whether she could ever forgive her father. But there was no time for that now.

'We already know what she's capable of.' Greg was speaking carefully too.

Cat felt a warm rush of thankful relief for the way he could understand so quickly. So different to Stephen, who was still shaking his head in denial in the back. She could see him in the mirror. 'Stop that, Stephen. Please. You're only distracting me.'

Greg said, 'If you let me drive, you can ring him and warn him to watch out for her.'

'Yes, you're right — Oh.' Almost at

once, Cat was shaking her head. 'That wouldn't work. He and I fell out big time when I told him I was going to marry Stephen. We haven't spoken since. He won't pick up.' She hesitated. 'If he even has his phone on. He forgets.'

'You never said,' Stephen interrupted.

'I did mention it — but I didn't make a big thing of it. Let's face it, you were quite relieved when I said he wouldn't be coming to the wedding.'

'I'll try phoning him, then.' Stephen suggested. 'If you give me my phone, Greg. If you feel you can trust me with it.'

Greg was already leaning over and passing it to him. Cat said, 'If he won't talk to me, he's even less likely to answer you. I'm sorry, Stephen, but he doesn't like you at all.'

For once, Cat thought, her dad — who often took unreasonable dislikes to people — had been right. *A pity I didn't listen to him. But then, I would never have met Greg, would I?*

The thought was like a tiny shimmer of sunlight.

'I'll try him.' Greg had his own phone in his hand now. 'Tell me the number.'

Cat already knew there would be no answer. She could hear the phone ringing out, uselessly. How many times had she told her father to keep his mobile phone on? Perhaps he wouldn't have gone far. Or maybe it would be better if he had; at least Amanda would have less chance of finding him. She sighed. 'Keep trying. Perhaps he'll turn it on eventually.'

'You're right,' Stephen announced suddenly. 'I'm not going to be any help with this after all. Let me out at the next services.'

Cat frowned. They had wasted enough time on Stephen already, but at least they would be rid of him. And he was hardly about to meet up with Amanda — she was obviously long past here and wouldn't be coming back for him.

An illuminated sign loomed in front of them.

'Queues ahead,' Greg pointed out. 'Dropping Stephen off won't take much of our time.' He was fiddling quickly with his phone. 'Tell you what, I've got a good route-finding app on here. Those queues are pretty long, must have been an accident or something. Don't bother with waiting for the services, take the next exit and we'll find a better route. We may even catch up with her.'

'Or get there first,' Cat said. And good — there was an exit just ahead. They weren't the only drivers taking advantage of it, although most people seemed to prefer to stay put and wait it out. Just as well.

She pulled into a lay-by to let her ex-fiancé out. With a cheery, 'Thanks, bye,' Stephen strode off.

Greg frowned. 'Didn't seem to bother him that we've just dumped him in the middle of nowhere.'

'Never mind about him. Where next?'

★ ★ ★

Amanda smiled to herself. At last. The stupid man had picked up.

'Ah, Mr Downes, I'm so glad I've got hold of you. It's Amanda Lewis. We used to be neighbours.' *And you had an affair with my mum and wrecked my life.*

Amanda was hardly surprised that his voice was cautious. 'What do you want?' But then he hurried on. 'Because if this is something to do with my daughter's wedding, I'm just not interested. She knows that. She's put you up to this, hasn't she? I don't want to hear about it. I told her what I thought and she wouldn't listen. I washed my hands of it.'

No sign at all of any guilt or remorse about what he'd done to the Lewis family. Why wasn't she surprised?

'No, no. Nothing like that. Please hear me out.' Amanda smiled to herself. 'Cat didn't want me to call you but I knew I had to. She needs to see you, Robert. She's very upset.'

She could picture him frowning.

'Go on.' Now he sounded uncertain. Suspicious, even.

'The wedding's off.'

'Ah. Can't say I'm sorry. I told her not to trust him, from the start.'

'You were right.'

'And she wants to see me? Has she said that? Because I told her what I thought of him and in no uncertain terms. I didn't hold back. And she didn't like it.' He paused again but this time, Amanda thought he was probably grinning, pleased with himself. 'And neither did he.'

'I know you and Cat fell out over it.' Amanda's voice was soft with understanding. 'She so wants to make it up with you. I can tell, though she can't bring herself to do it. I think she doesn't know how —— '

This sounded a bit far-fetched. Perhaps she was overdoing it. But no. Robert Downes sounded moved, almost emotional.

'There's no need for her to feel like

that. Of course I'll talk to her. Put her on.'

'I'm sorry, I can't. She isn't here. She doesn't even know I'm phoning you.'

'I see. Well, thanks for telling me. I'll ring her straight away. Don't worry. I'll sort it out.'

'No, no. Don't do that.' That would wreck everything. She had to keep him talking. Amanda breathed deeply though it was an effort to keep calm. The arrogance of the man! As if one word from him would make everything all right. 'I'll need to talk to her first. I'll have to try and persuade her to talk to you. We'll have to see if she'll agree to it.'

Knowing Cat and how soft she could be, she probably would — and forgive him too. Like a shot. Amanda grinned. An apt choice of simile there, considering what she had planned for him. Because Amanda would never forgive him. Never.

She suggested helpfully, 'Perhaps I can take you to meet her. A surprise reunion. Yes, I think that will be the best

291

way to play it.' She held her breath. Would he fall for it?

He paused. 'You mean, we won't let on until we get there? Yes, I can go with that. She'll need her old dad at a time like this. And you know what? I'll promise not to say *I told you so*.' He laughed.

Amanda sighed.

'Oh, I know. It's so tempting. That will be very difficult. For me too. But she needs our support.'

'That's great. Well, get yourself here and we can get going.'

'Thank you so much. This will be a weight off my mind, I can tell you.'

Not one word of doubt. Robert Downes was convinced he had been in the right all along. In fact, Amanda didn't think there was any real sympathy or feeling for Cat in his voice. No, he was cock-a-hoop at being proved right in his opinion of Stephen.

'Oh — and if Cat should happen to phone you herself, I think you should ignore it. Otherwise, it will spoil the surprise.'

'Yes, I will do.' He laughed again. 'She won't think anything of it. She's always telling me off for not having my phone on. I can't wait to see her face. And thank you — Amanda, isn't it? You're a true friend.'

'Oh, Mr Downes, you're embarrassing me,' Amanda trilled. Now she was overdoing it, surely — but she could hardly suppress her glee at how well her ploy was working. 'See you soon,' she said quickly, before she allowed herself to be carried away even further and ruined the whole thing. 'Be ready.'

She cancelled the call. *Just you wait, Robert Downes,* she thought. *Are you going to get what's coming to you? Aren't you just.*

★ ★ ★

'Still no answer,' Greg said. 'Perhaps he's out. Would he be at work?'

'Oh — yes.' Cat tried to sound cheerful. 'I'm sure that will be it. And I don't think I've ever told Amanda where he works. Why would I?'

She hoped against hope that she hadn't. But she hadn't known her father had been responsible for the dreadful division in Amanda's family. Every time she mentioned him, it must have been another wound in Amanda's heart — at least since Amanda had found out the truth herself.

Oh, why had Amanda never said anything? It would have been far better if they could have talked about it. No wonder Amanda was hurt and angry. Cat was angry with him too. At least she would be, when she had time to sit back and think it through . . .

'Careful,' Greg said as Cat braked to avoid the car in front. 'It's OK, you missed it. You're driving on autopilot and I can't blame you.'

'I'm just hoping we're in time.' Because she was almost certain her father would be in. He worked on his laptop at home mostly, only going into the office when he couldn't avoid it. He couldn't stand the traffic in the city centre and didn't feel he could rely on the trains.

She must stop thinking about anything else except the task in hand. She had to concentrate on driving. And getting there . . . in time.

By now they had left the motorway and every traffic light seemed to be against them. Every roundabout was clogged with queues. Cat could hardly sit still.

'It will have been the same for her,' Greg said.

Cat tried to smile.

'And I know the short cuts. As we get nearer.' She looked over her shoulder, indicating to change lanes. 'There's one coming up, too.'

For the next ten minutes, she was silent and Greg respected her mood. But the running commentary in her head was so negative that she was beginning to wish he would say something.

Then Greg said, 'Do we need a plan?'

'I suppose it depends on what we find. And what's happening. I'm hoping

I can talk her out of it. And get the gun off her.'

'How about you do the talking, I get the gun?'

Cat frowned, considering.

'Even better if she doesn't realise you're there. Assuming they're in the sitting room, you can wait in the hall. He's supposed to be knocking through and making it all open plan. He hasn't got round to it yet. Just as well.' She turned right at a familiar crossroads. 'He hasn't got round to doing much of anything since Mum died.'

'She must have meant a great deal to him.'

Cat sighed. 'I always thought so. And yet he could have an affair with Sharon Lewis. Next door. Amanda's mother,' she added. Had she ever really known her dad? 'Right. Here we are.' Her voice rose as she slipped into a parking space. 'And there's Dad's car! He's here.'

Greg was looking round. 'I can't see Amanda's car. Perhaps you've outrun her.'

Cat was glancing up and down the street, too. 'She could be here any minute. Quick.'

Greg followed as she ran up the steps and rang the bell. 'I've got a key. He won't hear if he's dozed off or something.' She was all fingers and thumbs, and this door was always a bit awkward but at last, yes, they were in. Cat stopped.

'What is it?' Greg breathed.

'It's too quiet. Dad? Dad, where are you? He always works with the radio on.' She ran in and out of the sitting room and the kitchen. 'He's not here.' Her legs felt weak with the strength of her relief. 'We've made it and he's out somewhere.'

He could have walked to the shop on the corner. He often did that when he'd forgotten something.

Greg was running upstairs. She heard his footsteps above, as he checked out the two bedrooms and the small bathroom. He called down to her, 'Nothing up here.'

Cat ran back to the front door and

peered up and down the street. No, of course there was no sign of him. She should have known there wouldn't be. She was clutching at straws.

She could hear Greg in the kitchen. He said quietly, 'He's left a mug of coffee here. It's still warm.'

Cat followed him, dipping her finger into the mug. She sighed. 'It doesn't look as if we got here first after all.' She straightened her shoulders. 'We have to decide what we're going to do about it. Presumably Amanda's taken him some-where.'

Greg nodded. 'I can't think of any other explanation. And I don't suppose his phone is any more likely to be switched on.'

Cat brightened. 'Yes, his phone! It's usually on the table or in the kitchen. And there's no sign of it. Quick, back to the car. We do have a chance.' She hesitated a little by the car and then hurried to the passenger side. 'Can you drive now, please?'

Greg leaped in beside her. 'Where to?'

Cat was peering at her phone.

'I set him up with an app so I could find his phone for him — even if it's switched off.'

'Useful.'

'Yes. Though I never thought it would be a lifesaver. Not like this.' She took a deep breath. 'Here we go. It's working. And they're not too far away.'

* * *

Robert Downes looked around as Amanda pulled up. He seemed puzzled.

'Why would Cat be here? These look like empty flats. Are they new?'

It was more than twenty years since he had recklessly split two families, uncaring of the hurt he was inflicting — but even with greying hair and a slightly loosening jawline, he was still insufferably handsome. Amanda's mother hadn't stood a chance.

She must be so careful to conceal her hatred.

'It's meant to be a surprise really.'

Amanda lowered her voice as if conveying a secret. 'So this is a bit naughty of me, I have to admit.'

How far could she spin this before he smelled a rat and she had to produce the gun? But so far, so good. He didn't seem suspicious at all.

'She's thinking of moving to Leeds, now it's all fallen through with Stephen. She wants a completely fresh start. And thought it would be good for her to be near you.' She unfastened her seat belt. 'Come on.'

He was shaking his head. Amanda's hand went to her bag. He turned to look at her, half smiling and she saw that far from being suspicious, his eyes were bright. He was actually emotional at the thought of Cat moving to be nearer him.

'That's kind of her. I haven't made too good a job of being on my own.'

'Well, you needn't worry about it any more.' Amanda's voice was brisk. She just had to get him inside, off the street. Once she had done what she had to do, making sure he knew why, he was unlikely to be discovered for some time.

These flats were deceptive. Whoever had been refurbishing the building had run out of money. No one had been near them for over a year. Quite a surprise that they hadn't been occupied by squatters — but lucky for her.

Unexpectedly, he reached out and gripped her arm. Amanda jumped.

'I'll bet it was you who suggested this to her, wasn't it? You were always kind, even as a child. I can't thank you enough.'

Amanda shook her head.

'Come on.' She looked up at the surrounding windows. Unlikely that anyone would be watching them, but you couldn't be too careful. No one had any idea that when she, too, had gone to view the building before the original auction, a couple of years ago, she had had the key copied. No one had cared.

He followed her inside like a lamb and up the stairs.

'It needs a lot doing to it as yet,

doesn't it? But I can help her with that. I expect she was counting on me. I shan't let her down.'

Sickeningly confident of his own charm.

'It's right at the top,' Amanda said. She avoided looking at him. Like a lamb to the slaughter. She knew her exultation was all too obvious. 'That one has the best views, over the rooftops across the road. That's why Cat chose it, of course.'

She opened the last door and gestured him inside.

He said, 'Cat? It's your dad — ' He paused. 'Where is Cat? I don't understand.' And he turned to face the gun Amanda was now pointing at his chest.

15

Greg pulled up behind Amanda's car and Cat led the way to the nearest door. It was standing open slightly. She edged round and into the dusty hall, a finger to her lips. Greg nodded. On one of the upper floors, they could hear voices.

She put her mouth close to Greg's ear.

'All we have is surprise. We'll do what we talked about earlier.'

Greg gave her a thumbs up and they began to creep up the stairs. The voices became more distinct, although Amanda seemed to be doing most of the talking.

As they reached the second floor of the Victorian building, they could make out most of what she was saying.

'You've had this coming to you. All the trouble you've caused. Without thinking about anyone else.'

A man's voice. 'But that was years

ago. It's all water under the bridge. You've done well for yourself, haven't you? You're all right now.'

Amanda's voice was low and threatening. It was impossible to tell what she had said.

Robert Downes was pleading.

'Come on, you can't be seriously thinking about using that on me. What would that achieve? Put it down, there's a good girl.'

Cat winced. At least he was all right so far. But not for long if he carried on like that. It was all she could do to keep her feet moving slowly and steadily without hurrying; they must not give themselves away.

The door at the top was open. She peered round it carefully. Neither her father nor Amanda was facing her.

Greg put a hand on her arm. She turned and smiled at him, reassuringly, but gesturing to him to stay back. She knew what she was going to do.

Greg mouthed, 'Cat! No.'

Cat strode out across the room. The

304

other two both stared at her.

Her father cried, 'Cat, get back. It's all right.'

'I know. It will be.'She stopped, facing Amanda. 'There's no need to do this. It won't help.'

Amanda glared at her.

'How do you know what will help me and how I feel? Why must you always interfere?'

'I need to save you from committing this crime. It will ruin your life.'

'My life was ruined as soon as he persuaded my mother to have an affair with him. Nothing was ever the same after that. Doing this will put things right. At last.'

'But there's no way you can possibly get away with this. It will be murder.'

'No, because with my plan no one would have known who did it. That's why we're here. No one will find him for weeks — months, even.' Amanda stopped. 'Or they wouldn't have done.'

Cat turned her back on her father, spreading her arms wide.

'Drop the gun, Amanda. I'm not moving. To shoot him, you'll have to shoot me too.'

Amanda hesitated.

From the door, Greg said, 'And me as well.'

As if in a sudden panic, Amanda swung the firearm from one to the other — and fired. The shot reverberated in the echoing space. Cat's throat constricted, and she gave a strangled cry. But they were all still standing.

Her relief was short-lived. Amanda had missed, but she was still holding the gun.

'Please, Amanda.' Cat reached forward. 'Give that to me.'

'And give up on having my revenge? No way. I've waited years for this. That shot was just to show you what I can do. And if I have to shoot both of you as well, I will. In fact, you've left me no choice.'

Below, the front door banged. They could all hear the running footsteps coming nearer.

'It's the police,' Cat said, thinking quickly. 'Drop the gun, Amanda, before they get here. Then you won't even be in possession of a firearm. There will be nothing to charge you with.'

'I don't believe you. I prefer to wait and see.' Was it Cat's imagination or was Amanda's voice less certain now?

Cat hoped it was the police — although she didn't see how it could be. Unless Greg had managed to call them? She wished she had thought about it. She had just been so intent on getting here.

The footsteps were pounding to the door. Greg stepped to one side as two figures threw themselves through it.

'Stephen!' Cat exclaimed in surprise. 'How did you get here?'

'With me.'

Had she seen this man before? Dark and thin-faced and yes, there seemed to be something familiar about him. Cat frowned. Of course — she had glimpsed him when Greg had given her a leg up to look over the Brystons' wall.

Amanda took a step back, her face white with shock. She was shaking.

'Vincent! But you're dead — Mike killed you.'

The gun fell from her hand, making a dull sound as it hit the floor. This time it was Greg who snatched it up.

'He thought he had.' Vincent didn't sound in the least like any of his brothers. His voice was warm and encouraging. Cat could understand why Greg would have agreed to work with him. 'But I'm fully recovered now.'

'And no crutches?' Greg had asked the question Cat was ready to ask.

'I haven't needed those for a while. But I had my reasons for continuing to use them. There was a great deal that needed sorting before I admitted to full health.' He grinned disarmingly.

'Sorting?' Greg queried.

'I didn't want Dean taking over again. You were right. Letting my brother get involved wasn't a good idea.'

'And there's other stuff.' Stephen burst into the conversation. 'Such as — we need to know — where is Vincent's laptop?'

Abruptly, all the fight seemed to have left Amanda. Her voice was sullen.

'In my flat. There are a couple of loose planks under the chest of drawers in the bedroom.'

'That's great, then. No problem.' Stephen was all smiles. 'I have a key to Amanda's flat, Vincent.'

'Wait a minute,' Cat interrupted. 'How did you get here?'

Stephen was still grinning.

'Vincent picked me up, of course, when you two dropped me off. And I've made a point of knowing where Amanda's phone is, since I moved in with her. Somehow, even though I loved her, I never quite trusted her.'

'And Vincent?' Greg said quietly. 'How did he come into it?'

'We had an arrangement,' Stephen went on. 'Because I managed to find out he was still alive and where he was.'

'You were holding out on me.' Greg was frowning. 'You knew how much that information would have meant to me.'

'No.' Vincent was shaking his head. 'It wasn't like that. He hasn't known long. And once we got back together, we agreed we had to discover who to trust, and exactly what had happened. With Stephen's help, I was beginning to piece together what I could remember about the attack.'

Stephen was hurrying on as if that hardly mattered to him.

'And Vincent and I are going to work together again. We've been discussing that on the way here. It's all sorted.'

'And without the dubious assistance of my relatives,' Vincent said. 'I'm afraid they've always been a bit over-enthusiastic.'

Stephen interrupted again. 'And since everything will be squeaky clean and above board now — that means you can come in with us just as before, doesn't it, Greg? We can carry on from where we left off. It's a bright, bright future.'

Cat sighed. Was this a future she

could have any part of, she wondered? No, not if she was going to follow her dream.

Had she ever wanted Greg for himself, however — or because he seemed to represent something she had always dreamed of? She closed her eyes and came to a new realisation.

If Greg was going to return to the busy and overwhelming world of business and city living, so be it. She would rather embrace that world again herself, even though it was the last thing she wanted, than lose him.

If he even wanted her in his life, that is.

Greg said, 'No.'

'What?' Stephen was dumbfounded.

'Thanks for the offer, both of you. But as I've already told Cat, I never realised how much I felt stifled by that entire dog-eat-dog world. I never want to go back to it. And you two can easily take over my part of it, without me.'

Stephen shook his head.

'I don't get it. What will you do instead?'

'I think I understand.' Vincent was nodding. 'I did a lot of thinking when I was recovering. I had plenty of time.'

'That's right. No doubt Mike's motive in getting me to conceal myself on the island that belonged to his parents was to keep me out of the way. Then I couldn't interfere with his plan of recovering the money he thought should be his. But I've never enjoyed myself so much, or been so at one with myself, knowing I was doing something so worthwhile.' He paused, smiling as if envisaging some secret inner happiness.

'Not only on the island; I came up with various ideas for protecting the environment on a larger scale. That's what I intend to do.'

Cat couldn't prevent the smile that was spreading across her face too. This would be so good for him. Her smile lapsed as she remembered how this was only one part of what needed to be sorted out.

Once again, Greg seemed to be reading her thoughts. He was still

312

standing close to Amanda and with the gun in his hand, although all the fight seemed to have left her now. He said, 'The police are on the way. I managed to call them when I was waiting outside.'

Cat closed her eyes briefly, taking a deep breath of relief. 'That's good. Thanks.' Something else occurred to her. 'But that means, Vincent, once they arrive you may get held up here making statements. You can't really add anything to what Greg and I can tell them, so I think you and Stephen should get back to the hut on the beach as quickly as possible to see what's happening down there.'

Vincent looked from her to Stephen and back.

'Why? What do you mean?'

'Whether the emergency services have arrived and what they've been able to do.' Cat looked at Stephen in disbelief. 'You haven't told him, have you? How could you do that?'

'We needed to discuss the business

and the money,' Stephen mumbled. 'I — didn't seem to get round to it.'

'Greg?' Vincent said.

Greg placed a hand on his shoulder and told him briefly what had happened to his brothers. Vincent's face was drained of all colour.

'I know they were a bad lot — but they're my family.'

Stephen said, quickly, 'I'll come with you. To show you where it is.'

'I suppose you'd better.'

They clattered down the stairs. Into the silence, Robert Downes said, 'I can't see those two working together after that.' He turned to face his daughter. 'You see, Cat, I was right about him, wasn't I? All along.'

Cat ignored him. That wasn't what she needed to hear just now. But he was her dad, funny and lovable and wildly irritating, just as he always had been — and she was so, so glad that they had reached him in time.

She said to Greg, 'Should we ring the police again and say we'll bring

314

Amanda in? That the situation is dealt with now?'

Greg said, 'Too late. I can hear the sirens.'

*   *   *

They stood together overlooking the sea, their backs to the newly repaired cottages. Once again, the sun was shining over the impossible expanse of blue. A faint breeze ruffled Cat's hair. She could hardly believe it was possible to feel so happy.

'This is where I first saw you — when I woke up. You were down on the beach,' she murmured.

Greg turned to smile at her.

'And when I first saw you, several hours before, you were slumped on my doorstep.'

'Yes. Left by Mike, as we know now. He was the mysterious man with a beard Amanda roped in to further her schemes — and to remove me from the bar.'

'Lucky for me that she did. And that he chose to bring you here.'

'Lucky for me too.' And that Mike's warped motivations had actually worked against him in the end. But none of that mattered now. 'We have to look to the future. And it's everything I have ever wanted. Working to keep this beautiful place and its environment safe for the future.'

'Yes. There's a lot to do, but it's all going to be worth it.'

She smiled up at him. 'And best of all is that we'll be doing this together.'

Yes — as their lips met she knew she had dreamed of this moment from the first time she had seen him, silhouetted against the sea. But now the dream was real.

We do hope that you have enjoyed reading this large print book.

Did you know that all of our titles are available for purchase?

We publish a wide range of high quality large print books including:
Romances, Mysteries, Classics
General Fiction
Non Fiction and Westerns

Special interest titles available in large print are:
The Little Oxford Dictionary
Music Book, Song Book
Hymn Book, Service Book

Also available from us courtesy of Oxford University Press:
Young Readers' Dictionary
(large print edition)
Young Readers' Thesaurus
(large print edition)

For further information or a free brochure, please contact us at:
Ulverscroft Large Print Books Ltd.,
The Green, Bradgate Road, Anstey,
Leicester, LE7 7FU, England.
Tel: (00 44) **0116 236 4325**
Fax: (00 44) **0116 234 0205**

WHAT THE HEART WANTS

Suzanne Ross Jones

Alistair is looking for a very particular kind of wife: a country girl who would be happy to settle down to life on his farm in the small town of Shonasbrae. Bonnie, fresh from the city to open her first of many beauty salons, isn't looking for a husband and she certainly isn't accustomed to country life. With such conflicting goals, Alistair and Bonnie couldn't be less compatible. But romance doesn't always make sense, and incompatible as the two are, they don't seem to be able to stay apart . . .

THE JADE TURTLE

Margaret Mounsdon

When Jack and Alice split up, he broke not only her heart, but also their business partnership. Running their agency alone, Alice discovers that Lan Nguyen had, unbeknownst to her, contracted Jack to steal a jade turtle. Unable to refund Lan, Alice is expected to take on the job herself. Reluctant to commit theft, she finds an unexpected ally in Jack's brother Mike. Then somebody else steals the turtle first — and Alice and Mike must find out who!

HER FORGOTTEN LOVE

Elizabeth McGinty

When Elisa catches her partner in bed with another woman, she sets off for Italy to stay with her grandfather Stephano. Greeted at Verona airport by her childhood friend Cesare — now a handsome policeman — she learns that Stephano is ill in hospital, and just manages to see him before he passes away. Then she finds out that he has left her his beloved hotel. Can she make a new life for herself in Italy — perhaps with Cesare by her side?

SUSIE'S SCARE

Adelaide Jolley

Susie Cotting thought Lex Maceul was the one and only boy for her. But when he was away doing his National Service with the RAF, he suddenly stopped replying to her letters ... Two years later, Susie is focused on her own life: working in her mother's shop and taking evening classes. She's convinced herself she's over her heartbreak. Then Lex comes back on two months' leave — and Susie discovers she isn't over him at all!